Dear Romance Reader,

Welcome to a world of breathtaking passion and never-ending romance.
Welcome to *Precious Gem Romances*.

It is our pleasure to present *Precious Gem Romances*, a wonderful new line of romance books by some of America's best-loved authors. Let these thrilling historical and contemporary romances sweep you away to far-off times and places in stories that will dazzle your senses and melt your heart.

Sparkling with joy, laughter, and love, each *Precious Gem Romance* glows with all the passion and excitement you expect from the very best in romance. Offered at a great affordable price, these books are an irresistible value—and an essential addition to your romance collection. Tender love stories you will want to read again and again, *Precious Gem Romances* are books you will treasure forever.

Look for fabulous new *Precious Gem Romances* each month—available only at Wal★Mart.

Kate Duffy
Editorial Director

FOOL FOR LOVE

Megan Byrne

ZEBRA BOOKS

Kensington Publishing Corp.

http://www.zebrabooks.com

ZEBRA BOOKS are published by

Kensington Publishing Corp.
850 Third Avenue
New York, NY 10022

Zebra and the Z logo Reg. U.S. Pat. & TM Off.

First Printing: April, 2000
10 9 8 7 6 5 4 3 2 1

Printed in the United States of America

To Bill and Jimmy,
for making all my dreams come true.

Special thanks to Tina Tsallas,
my agent at Great Titles,
for her input and encouragement.

One

"You told your aunt *what?*" Kitty O'Neill stared across the kitchen table at her best friend, positive she had heard wrong.

"I told her you'd start next week." Beth Lawson scooped up the photographs scattered on the table-top and calmly stacked them into one neat pile. "Aunt Helen was leaving for Boca Raton and wanted everything settled."

"So you told her I agreed to do the job?" It was a huge presumption, even for Beth, who was naturally impulsive. "What if I don't want it?"

"You can't turn it down, Kitty. This job is perfect for you. Aunt Helen wants the best restoration specialist I could find. Nobody knows Victorian architecture like you do!" Beth fumbled through the stack of photos and selected two at random. "Here," she said, passing them across the table. "Look at these pictures again. Have you ever seen a place more beautiful than Lakeview Manor?"

"It is a beautiful estate," Kitty agreed. "But—"

"And look at the woodwork. The whole west wing of the manor is loaded with fancy trim. Just how you like it. You're the only one I know who can miter cornices to perfection. In all honesty, Kitty, how can you say no?"

"Well, for starters, Beth, your aunt lives in Lake George, New York. We live in Philadelphia. I see a problem with logistics right there."

Beth shrugged as if the three hundred mile distance didn't faze her in the least. "So? The idea is to spend the summer there. I've arranged to take a few weeks off from work to help you out. It'll be just like old times, Kit!" Her brown eyes sparkled with excitement at the idea. "And you know you could use a change of scenery."

Kitty couldn't argue with that. The past few months since her divorce had been very stressful. It would be nice to get away. Even to work.

She leaned back in her chair, thinking of all the arrangements she'd have to make if she accepted the job. She'd have to sublet her apartment, for one thing. And postpone some of the small jobs she had taken on.

"Aunt Helen will pay you top dollar. And even a little extra to make it worth your while." Beth withdrew a sheet of paper from her purse and handed it across the table. "I've got the contract right here. Read it over. I'm authorized to give you a deposit now."

Kitty eyed the contract. "It is an attractive offer," she agreed quietly. One that she couldn't afford to pass up. In fact, a job like that would be like a gift from heaven—far better than any other work she had lined up for the summer. And there were so many bills to pay, another installment due on her business loan, the lease on her utility truck . . .

Her debts, it seemed, were endless.

Kitty swallowed a sigh of impatience. Her current financial problems were only temporary. She had to remember that. Starting up her own business required a lot of capital. That was understandable. And even though Jay Hilliard had drained every last penny from her bank account before their divorce, she'd get back on her feet again.

She ground her teeth against the wave of anger that surged at the thought of her ex-husband and the mountain of unpaid bills and obligations he had dumped on her. Renovating the west wing of Helen Brody's old Victorian house would be a healthy start at shrinking those debts.

"Kitty . . ." Beth began, concerned. "Money isn't the only reason to take the job. You need to go someplace where Jay can't . . . find you."

"We're divorced now, Beth."

"You think that matters? You think the next time he's strapped for money he won't come to you first?"

Kitty tried to shrug off Beth's fears. "Even Jay knows when to quit. He has no legal right to anything of mine. I'm sure he won't bother me." She glanced away, frowning. Their divorce was final, but she still found herself looking over her shoulder, half expecting Jay to show up.

Just bad memories, she thought, subduing a shiver. "And anyway, Beth," she continued, trying to keep a positive outlook, "Jay left town after the divorce.

For all I know he's moved away. He could be anywhere by now."

"He's not." Beth's voice was grim. "I think I saw him walking out of the Ritz Carlton last week. Maybe I'm wrong, Kitty, but I have a bad feeling about him. You know how long it took him to agree to the divorce settlement and sign those papers. He thought he should have had more money." She shook her head firmly. "I don't trust him to stay away from you. That's why you need to come to Lake George. You'll be out of his reach for three months."

Kitty knew Beth was right. Divorce or no divorce, Jay would come calling just as soon as he needed something.

He'd never find her at Lakeview Manor, though. She could relax her guard, have a worry-free summer.

"So what do you think?" Beth glanced at her watch. "I've got to get back to work. Are you interested?"

"A Victorian manor all to ourselves for the summer?" It was too tempting to turn down. Kitty set the contract on the table and smiled at Beth. "Where do I sign?"

Beth grinned and handed her a pen. "You're going to *love* Lakeview Manor!"

"Are you sure the key is missing?" The deep male voice broke through the stillness of the elegant, antique-filled foyer of Lakeview Manor.

Harold Sugarman motioned to the old mahogany credenza. "It's always been kept in that top drawer," he reminded his boss. "I noticed the drawer was empty."

Keefe Brody forced himself to keep calm. "Was anything else taken?"

"I don't think so. I checked the entire house." Harold frowned, his gray eyebrows drawing together in a single, bushy line. "They got in through the solarium—left a window open. All kinds of rain blowing in!" he muttered, shaking his head. "The woodwork is water damaged as it is. Mrs. Brody was complaining about it just last week before she left." He rubbed the back of his neck and sighed. "I'm sorry, sir. If I'd been here . . ."

"Don't worry about it, Hal," Keefe said reassuringly. "You're only here once or twice a week. It's not your job to police the property. I should have been here myself."

Keefe was grateful that only the key had been taken. Last month, on one of his mother's jaunts to Florida, someone had broken in and taken a few pieces of jewelry before Harold's arrival had frightened him off. So much more could easily have been stolen. With his mother down in Boca Raton, Keefe knew he'd been foolish to stay away.

Still, he couldn't help but wonder about the missing key. Whoever stole it intended to return. He'd bet on it.

"So what do we do now?"

Keefe gave the caretaker an affectionate smile and clapped him on the shoulder. "Go on home to your wife, Hal. It's six-thirty. You've stayed much later than usual."

Harold looked worried. "I don't feel right leaving the manor unoccupied."

"It won't be. I'll be here for the summer." Now that spring term was over, spending the next few months at Lakeview Manor would be no problem. The timing was perfect.

Relief softened Harold's face. He glanced hesitantly at his boss. "Will Miss Gallagher be joining you?"

"Liz and I aren't seeing each other anymore."

"Oh, sir . . ." Harold fumbled for the right words. "I'm sorry . . ."

The half-hearted apology had Keefe grinning. "No, you're not." He knew the old caretaker wasn't too fond of anyone who complained of persistent boredom at Lakeview Manor. "And to be honest, Hal, I'm not sorry either. I'm actually looking forward to spending the summer alone here." A few months of quiet solitude was just the thing he needed after a hectic school year. No classes to teach, and, he told himself firmly, no women. He'd had it with dating for a good long while. In fact, if he didn't see a single woman for the entire summer, it was fine with him.

The thought of the weeks of freedom that stretched out ahead of him had Keefe sighing with pleasure. This summer he'd spend his vacation doing what he wanted. He'd finally put some serious time into the book he was forever working on and get his old canoe back into the lake.

He smiled at the caretaker as he handed him his windbreaker from the coat rack in the corner. "So you see, Hal, I won't be distracted from keeping watch here."

"What if the thief comes back?"

Keefe shrugged negligently. "I'll handle it."

Harold studied his boss, concerned. Indeed, the broad-shouldered professor of American History looked more than capable of handling it. But trying to apprehend the criminal himself would be too risky.

"You will call the police, won't you? If anything happens? With all due respect, sir, you're not Batman."

Keefe's laughter rang out in the foyer. "I'm crushed, Hal. There goes my childhood dream of being a superhero."

"I'm being quite serious . . ."

Keefe sobered. He had known the old caretaker all his life. Harold Sugarman was nothing if not loyal. "I know you're serious. And I appreciate your concern."

"Then humor me, sir. Let the police fight crime." He slipped into his jacket and adjusted the collar. "You promise you'll call them?"

"Sure." But Keefe was grinning again as he walked Harold to the door. "What's the number for 911?"

Harold shook his head and gave a loud groan.

Kitty parked her utility truck behind Beth's car and shut off the motor. Excited at her first glimpse of Lakeview Manor, she climbed down from the driver's seat and hurried over to Beth. "It's beautiful!" she gushed.

"It looks haunted, doesn't it?"

Kitty glanced at her friend in amusement. "You're being silly, Beth. It doesn't look haunted, just . . . lonely. Nobody's home. This house is a perfect example of Victorian architecture. It's a renovator's dream come true. Look at the intricate carving along the roofline!"

"Told you you'd love it."

"Well, I can't wait to look around." The bright May sun had dipped behind the rolling peaks of the Adirondacks. Thick, gray clouds loomed on the horizon to the south. Night was approaching fast, and maybe a storm, too, from the looks of the sky. She wouldn't have much time to explore outside.

"Let's go back to town before we get settled," Beth said. "I'm starving."

Kitty stared longingly at the house. She didn't want to leave Lakeview Manor after spending so many hours behind the wheel to get there. "I'm not hungry."

"So stay here. I'll go pick up some groceries." Beth grabbed a key from her purse and handed it to Kitty. "Here. You can let yourself in. I'll be back before you know it," she promised as she climbed back into her car.

Thunder rumbled ominously in the distance as Beth drove off. Kitty ignored it, turning back to study the old house and its wealth of Victorian decorative detail. Gingerbread latticework trimmed the roofline while graceful scrollwork added a fanciful edge to the peaked gables. A pair of stone turrets flanked the center entrance of the manor like tall bookends. Jutting from each turret like welcoming arms were the east and west wings.

The house was solid and strong, built into the gentle slope of the terrain, as much a part of the natural landscape as the hills and woods. The whole effect was one of stability, a house that had witnessed the turn of the century, weathered the tests of time, and offered its occupants the shelter and comfort of a loving embrace.

A small sigh escaped Kitty's lips. For the first time since her divorce, she felt optimistic about the future. The tension that normally held her neck and shoulders in a painful grip slowly melted away.

A sudden clap of thunder startled her out of her thoughts. She scurried up the steps and unlocked the door, just as the first drops of rain began to fall.

Kitty shoved the key in the pocket of her jeans and stepped into the foyer. She spotted a light switch and snapped it on. The room lit up with a warm, soft glow.

"Looking for something?"

A deep, masculine voice came at her out of nowhere. Kitty turned and let out a startled gasp. He stood by the stairway, tall and grim-faced, watching her through narrowed eyes. In his hand was a large silver vase.

The shock of his sudden appearance sent an electric jolt to her heart. Lakeview Manor was supposed to be empty. That left only one possibility. She eyed the silver vase, comprehension dawning.

The man had broken in. She'd interrupted a burglar.

Kitty didn't bother answering him. She bolted for the door.

Keefe set down the vase and lunged after her, mentally dismissing Hal's prior urging to call the police. He'd handle this little intruder himself. No problem.

He reached her just as her hand brushed the doorknob.

Kitty screamed as his arm snaked around her waist. Without a word, he lifted her off her feet and headed for the hallway leading to the back of the house.

Kitty squirmed and pushed at his arm, trying to dislodge his tight grip. Instead, he drew her closer and continued down the darkened hallway, stopping to turn through a doorway on the right. With a brisk stride, he carried her to a leather couch and sat her down.

Lightning flickered and the lights dimmed. A loud volley of thunder battered the air like a drum roll, rattling the windowpanes. But it was the deep growl of the man's voice that made Kitty jump nervously.

"This is a surprise." He was gazing down at her with curiosity, his green eyes, she was relieved to see, holding no hint of a threat. "You're not at all what I expected."

He was expecting someone? Kitty eyed him cautiously. He seemed even bigger now than he had at first. His hair was thick and black, shoved in a careless sweep off his forehead, long enough to touch the neck of his white T-shirt. Good heavens, she thought suddenly. All the man needed was an earring and a cutlass between his teeth and he'd pass for a pirate.

Keefe conducted a little appraisal of his own. Having a woman break into his home was the last thing he expected. And she was pretty, too, her sunny blond hair and wide blue eyes making him think of summer days and cloudless skies. Not breaking and entering.

Wait a minute.

What the hell was he doing? He should be interrogating her, not noticing how pretty she was.

"Get comfortable," he ordered. "We're going to have a little talk, you and I." He strode over to his desk and snapped the lamp on before returning to glare at her. The fact that his thief was a woman didn't lessen the severity of the crime. But as she stared up at him, her lower lip trembled slightly before she caught it between her teeth. Another blast of guilt hit him. He'd probably frightened the hell out of her. And looking at her mouth had definitely been a big mistake. He was suddenly filled with an uncontrollable urge to kiss away her fear.

He shook his head and turned to face the windows, watching lightning flicker beyond the dark glass. "What were you intending to take this time?" he asked harshly. "Money? More jewelry?"

Kitty blinked at him, bewildered. "What?"

He looked back at her, frowning. "Don't play games. I know you have the key to the house. Quite useful for a small-time thief to take, wouldn't you say?"

"You actually think I'm here to—!" Kitty couldn't have been more surprised if he had accused her of coming from Mars. If she hadn't been so scared, she might have laughed. "I'm not here to cut in on your action, if that's what you're worried about."

"I'm no burglar." He raised one dark brow. "And I'll be damned if I let one rob my mother's house again."

Beth hadn't said one word about Mrs. Brody having a son. Kitty knew her friend wouldn't omit such an important fact. He had to be lying. "I don't believe you."

"Trust me," he said. "If I was a burglar, I'd be punishing you for catching me in the act. You'd be tied up by now . . ." He paused, his gaze dipping down the length of her and then back up. "Or worse."

His comment seemed to stop her heart. But her mind raced on, conjuring up a horrifying image. And the man looked more than capable of doing anything. "What—what a ridiculous thing to say," she said weakly.

"Is it?"

For the first time he smiled at her, and Kitty felt as if the floor had just dropped out from under her. The man was remarkably handsome when he smiled like that.

"Why don't you hand over the key you stole?"

His erroneous assumption had Kitty jumping to her feet in exasperation. Planting her hands on her hips, she stated, "I did not steal the key!"

He leaned down toward her until she could feel the warmth of his body and catch the faint scent of his aftershave.

"Then how did you get it?" he asked softly, his

breath stirring the strands of hair at her temple. His mouth was just an inch away, near enough for an impulsive kiss.

Kitty's heart thumped. That thought had come out of nowhere, rattling her nerves, sending her temperature soaring.

"I . . . Beth Lawson gave me the key," she stated hastily, trying to ignore the spark of sexual awareness that sizzled through her. Good God, what was the matter with her?

If she had expected her explanation to satisfy him, she was mistaken. He held his hand out for the key. Kitty had no doubt he'd grab it from her pocket himself if she didn't hand it over. Blushing at that thought, she fumbled in her pocket and gave it to him.

"Beth Lawson gave you the key," he repeated slowly, trying to make sense of it. Dammit, what was his cousin up to now? It would be just like her to loan Lakeview Manor to a vacationing friend.

He tossed the key to the top of the desk where it skittered over papers and clanged against the computer keyboard parked at the edge. "How do you know Beth?"

"We're friends. I'm Kitty O'Neill."

He shrugged off her name. "Doesn't ring a bell."

"Should it?" She set her jaw, riled by his dismissive attitude. "Beth never mentioned anything about *you.*"

"I'm her cousin. Keefe Brody." He exhaled impatiently. "You're lucky I didn't wring your neck first and then ask questions. I thought you were a burglar."

"Do I look like one?" she demanded irritably. "You should be ashamed, scaring me to death like that!"

"Sorry." He was grinning at her.

Kitty straightened her rumpled sweatshirt, anger burning away the last traces of fear. He wasn't sorry in the least. "We'll see what Beth has to say about this!" She crossed her arms, her expression mutinous.

That seemed to amuse him more. "I hate to disappoint you, Miss O'Neill, but if you're here to spend your vacation lazing about the manor, you've come for nothing. Beth has no authority in this house, not while I'm here."

"That's where you're wrong." Kitty allowed herself a small smile, feeling as though she held the winning ace. "I was hired to work here. On Beth's recommendation."

His smile disappeared. "What sort of work?"

"Detail carpentry, mostly."

"That's the first I've heard about it." His eyes roved over her, measuring her worth, his expression clearly one of disbelief.

Flustered, Kitty rushed to explain. "I'm here to repair some wainscoting. And trim work. And, um, crown molding. Some . . . uh, painting, too. That sort of thing. In the west wing." Without being aware of it, Kitty moved her hands as she talked, a nervous habit she had picked up as a child when she was feeling uneasy.

Keefe Brody was smiling again, noticing her discomfort and enjoying it in a perverse way. There was something about the seriousness in her big, blue eyes, the small hands that gestured as she talked, the defensive set to her shoulders, he found appealing. He eyed her, fascinated. "You're really a carpenter, huh?"

"Yes." She lifted her chin, acutely conscious of the man's eyes drifting over her body. "Beth's Aunt Helen—your mother—wanted some restoration work done while she was away. Apparently you weren't informed."

"How like Mother." He folded his arms, eager to pursue the matter further. "So you're here because Beth thought maybe you could do the job."

Kitty felt insulted. "I *can* do the job."

"That's a matter of opinion.

Her eyes narrowed. "What's that supposed to mean?"

"It means, Beth must be out of her mind."

Heat rose in her cheeks. She stood silently, unable to form a comeback, her fingers curling into tight fists.

"So I'm afraid you've come here for nothing."

"Not for nothing," she insisted. "For a job. And I'm staying put until Beth returns to confirm it."

He shrugged. "Fine. But you're wasting your time. You can't possibly . . ." He stopped, taking note of her clenched fists, and chuckled softly.

Kitty's temper rose. No one had ever laughed at her! Skepticism, yes. But laughter? Never. She drew herself up, affronted. "Why don't you just say it," she demanded coolly. "You don't think I'm capable, do you?"

"That's exactly what I think."

She stared at him, dumbfounded to hear him admit it so easily. She had been doing renovation work for years. Her carpentry skills were nothing less than impeccable. Hard, physical labor was business as usual to her. And yet the concept of her doing the work in the west wing had made him laugh.

"You shouldn't judge people you don't know."

"I know enough already." He gestured toward her with a sweep of his hand. "Just look at you. You're not the type for rough construction," he pronounced. "You're too small." His green eyes crinkled with humor as he pictured her trying to slap up drywall. "Even your name is all wrong. *Kitty.* Sounds like a cute piece of fluff to me."

Kitty's temper did a slow burn. She could ignore the insulting crack about her name, but to have him dismiss her on the basis of size alone was something she wouldn't tolerate. So what if she was just a smidgen under five-feet-four? What she lacked in height she more than made up in ambition and determination.

He gave her another once-over, lingering on small shoulders and slim hips. "You don't have the muscle to haul two-by-fours, much less work with power tools. My God, *you* with a power tool? A circular saw would run away with you!" He looked at her, suddenly curious. "I'll bet you don't even know what that is."

"Of course I do," Kitty quickly assured him. "I also know what a router is, and a radial saw, a scroll saw, a band saw, and a jigsaw. I've used every—" She saw his eyes twinkle with amusement and broke off, horrified at having been so easily goaded.

She didn't have to take this. She could argue and plead her case until she was blue in the face. There was just no convincing this chauvinistic man. The opinion he had formed of her had obviously been set in stone.

Without another word, she turned on her heel and headed out of the room, taking slow, deep breaths to calm herself. The man infuriated her with a maddening ease. She needed distance to regain control. Most of all, she needed Beth to call off her obnoxious cousin.

As though a magic wand had been waved, her wish was granted. The front door burst open.

Two

"What a storm!" Beth swept in on a gust of wind and slammed the door behind her. With a look of utter disgust she began plucking at her rain-splattered blouse. "I'm soaked!"

"You do look like a drowned mouse."

Beth's head popped up at the sound of her cousin's voice. A happy cry sprang from her lips. "Keefe! What brings you here?" She hurried over and gave him a quick hug, laughing as she dampened his shirt.

"Thought I'd better keep an eye on the place with mother in Florida. Someone broke in here just last month," he said. "Some jewelry was stolen."

"I heard about that," Beth said, her expression tightening in anger. "Has any of it been recovered?"

Keefe shook his head. "I'm sure the items have been pawned by now." He grinned at Kitty. "I thought your friend was the thief coming back for more."

Beth laughed at the idea of Kitty being taken for a burglar.

"It wasn't funny," Kitty said, glowering at them.

"Oh, don't worry, Kit," Beth said. "He doesn't bite."

One brow lifted as Keefe gazed at Kitty with a look of pure male arrogance. "Not unless she wants me to." He growled softly and bared his teeth for her benefit.

The deep, rumbling sound of that growl seemed to resonate through her. Kitty felt as though a flash fire had just raced across her skin. Disturbed at her reaction, she took a slow breath of air and gave him a cool look.

His antics made Beth laugh. "You see why his students love him so?" She patted him fondly on the arm. "Dr. Keefe Brody. Most popular professor in Albany."

Kitty didn't share Beth's biased opinion. The man was rude and irritating. And he was a *professor?* A man responsible for molding the youth of America? The country was in serious trouble indeed!

"So what's this about renovation work?" Keefe asked, turning back to Beth. "This is the first I've heard of it."

"Well, no wonder! Maybe if you talked to your mother more often, she would have told you. Honestly, what's so hard about picking up the phone once in a while?"

Keefe laughed. "Obviously, sweet cousin, you haven't eavesdropped on one of our conversations."

"It's about your bachelor status, isn't it?" Beth teased. "She wants a grandchild."

"Tell me about it," he said, sounding weary. "I told her if she couldn't pick another topic to discuss, I wouldn't call her."

"Bravo!" Beth exclaimed with a hearty laugh. "Nobody stands up to Aunt Helen."

"That's what scares me."

"Why?" she asked, sobering instantly. "She won't do anything spiteful, will she?"

"I don't know," he admitted. "But I do wonder about her sudden interest in renovating the west wing."

"Oh, that." Beth waved off Keefe's worry. "She decided to repair the wainscoting in the solarium. Everything had warped from those leaky old windows. And she wanted to fix up the playroom and nursery."

"Why bother?" Keefe gave a derisive snort. "Those rooms aren't used anyway."

And there was little prospect of them being used in the near future. Especially the nursery, for crying out loud. What was his mother thinking?

Oh, he knew what she was thinking. She wanted him to marry and raise a family. And he would. Eventually. But only if the right woman came along. He wanted someone who loved Lakeview Manor as much as he did. Someone who didn't mind life in the country—the quiet isolation, the slower pace. Until then, he was in no hurry.

"She offered no explanations," Beth told him. "I'm just doing her a favor hiring someone to do the work while she's in Florida. I'll call to get more details. So you won't have to," she added with a smirk.

"I'll owe you one." Keefe reached out and tousled Beth's short brown hair.

"So how long will you be staying? Are you teaching any classes this summer?"

"No," he answered. "I'm working on a biography of General John Burgoyne, specifically his role in the

Revolutionary War and the effects it had on the Adirondack area. I'll be here for the summer."

"The summer?" Kitty questioned loudly. Beth had assured her they'd have the manor to themselves. But *he'd* be here? A man who seemed to doubt whether she knew the business end of a hammer? Lakeview Manor was a big house, but not big enough to avoid Keefe Brody.

He seemed amused by her distress. "You can't expect me to leave the manor unsupervised now."

"I don't need supervision."

"We'll see. Beth might have been a little impulsive in hiring you. But I'll have to trust her judgment and let you stay." His lips curved in a sardonic smile. "Until the job becomes more than you can handle. And in my opinion, that shouldn't take too long."

"Nobody asked for your opinion," Kitty said through her teeth, anger flaring. So this was how it was going to be. Condescension and insults all summer long.

By God, she wouldn't listen to it! She brushed past Keefe and walked out the door, closing it behind her with a resounding bang.

Keefe stared after her for a moment, then turned to find Beth glaring forbiddingly at him. "What?" he asked with an innocent shrug.

"Was that really necessary?" She hadn't missed the animosity that had sparked like a live wire between her two favorite people.

Keefe ignored the question and asked one of his own. "My mother wanted you to hire someone, and you chose Kitty O'Neill?" The thought of his beloved manor in the unskilled hands of some slip of a woman made his head throb.

"Yeah. What's wrong with that?"

"She thinks she's a carpenter."

Beth gave a snort of impatience. "She *is* a carpenter. Give her a chance, Keefe. She can handle the job. Besides, she needs the money."

"Ahh . . ." Keefe said reflectively. "The real reason."

"That's not the only reason. She—"

"Look, I don't care what she needs," he cut in. "I don't think she can handle the work. Now I'll have to waste time keeping an eye on her."

A corner of Beth's mouth lifted in amusement as she headed to the kitchen. "You've already had an eye on her."

"Why didn't you warn me about him?" Kitty demanded later, pacing back and forth across the kitchen while Beth busied herself unpacking the groceries. "I thought you said Lakeview Manor would be empty when we got here!"

"So I was wrong," Beth returned with a small lift of her shoulder. She took out a can of coffee and a package of coffee filters from the grocery bag and put them away in the cupboard. "I don't see why you're so upset."

"He treated me like I was a burglar, for Pete's sake," Kitty explained, making a grimace of exasperation. "Believe me, he was not happy to see some stranger come strolling through the door with the house key."

Beth continued putting items away, humming a tune as she moved from kitchen table to cupboard to refrigerator, all while Kitty vented her anger. "Here, stick these in the freezer." She handed Kitty a bag of frozen bagels. "I was thinking of sandwiches for dinner. Okay? I bought some sliced ham and fresh rolls."

Kitty shoved the bagels in the freezer. "You haven't heard a word I said." Here she was, practically attacked by someone who looked as if he could bench press a piano and her best friend cared more about food. "I could have been assaulted. Beaten up!"

Beth gave a shout of laughter. "By Keefe?" She turned to give Kitty her full attention. "Judging from how he was looking at you, I'd say he'd be more inclined to smother you with kisses than do anything else."

Kitty held up a hand in warning. "I already regret taking this job. Don't make it any worse." But her friend's imagination was contagious. The all-too-real picture of Keefe Brody smothering her with kisses kicked her heart into a staccato beat.

Beth sighed as she folded the empty grocery bags and put them away. "All right," she relented. "I'm sorry he was here to surprise you."

"Surprise? He scared me to death! I thought he was some—some criminal. I tried to fight him off . . ."

"Oh, Kitty!" Beth said with an astonished laugh. "He's got a good twelve inches on you. And a hundred pounds, easy." She moved forward in concern, laying a gentle hand on Kitty's arm. "He didn't hurt you, did he?"

"No." Kitty shook her head. "But when he carried me into the study, you can imagine how—"

Beth gasped. "He swept you off your feet!" She took a step back, staring in awe at Kitty. "That is so romantic!"

"There was nothing romantic about it!" Kitty exploded, glaring at Beth as if she had lost her mind. "For heaven's sake, Beth, he thought I was here to rob the place!"

Beth tapped her foot, her face rapt with excited attention. "What happened next?"

Kitty glanced away, a telltale flush still on her cheeks. "Nothing."

"Nothing?" Beth looked disappointed.

"Well . . . I mean, he asked me my name, what I was doing here, things like that."

"And that's when you told him I hired you to come."

"Yes." Kitty decided to leave it at that. She would never admit to her friend that her pride had been wounded when Keefe had laughed at the idea of her doing renovation work. Beth would say she was being too sensitive.

Beth assembled the sandwiches and poured two glasses of iced tea, all while chattering with endless enthusiasm about her cousin. As they sat down at the oak table in the corner of the kitchen, Beth concluded her glowing report. "And best of all, he just broke up with his last girlfriend. He's available! What do you think about *that?*"

"Not much," Kitty replied. "Whether he's available or not has nothing to do with me. So don't get any ideas. We may be staying in the same house for the summer, Beth, but the renovation work will keep me more than busy." With that said, Kitty bit into her sandwich, hoping she had derailed Beth's train of thought once and for all.

Beth, however, remained stubbornly on track. "But you have to admit he is gorgeous, isn't he? And now that I've seen you both together, I think you make a great-looking couple. You, so blonde and petite and pretty, and Keefe so tall and dark and muscular. You complement each other. Like two pieces of a puzzle that fit together." She leaned her elbows on the table and sighed, her sandwich forgotten for the moment, her brown eyes soft and dreamy. "You're perfect for each other. All those years I've known you. I wonder why it never occurred to me before . . ."

Kitty rolled her eyes. "Just eat your dinner!"

They finished their meal in silence.

The high-pitched scream of a circular saw had Keefe gritting his teeth as he struggled to concentrate on his work. When the noise of the saw finally stopped, there was a loud crash as lumber hit the floor, followed by the relentless sound of banging.

He gave an audible groan. How the hell could he manage to write even one intelligible sentence with this racket going on? He ran a hand through his hair and sighed wearily, glancing at the clock on the mantle. Nine-thirty.

Why was she working *now*?

The hammering continued unabated. Keefe muttered an oath and rose to his feet. His pretty little carpenter had to be insane to be working this late at night. But she wasn't going to make a habit of it all summer long. Not if he had anything to say about it.

He headed into the hallway and followed the sound of hammering straight into the solarium. Kitty was pounding away to her heart's content, fashioning a crude sawhorse out of some scrap two-by-fours.

The room was dark except for the beam of a portable halogen light she had set up to illuminate the area around her.

Keefe could bet that Kitty had no idea how the bright halogen bulb highlighted her figure, casting a curvaceous silhouette against the wall. His attention drawn to the movement of her shadow, he forgot for a moment why he had come.

She stopped hammering suddenly and eyed him curiously. "Is something wrong?"

Keefe walked into the room, stepping into her circle of light. "I wanted to find out what all the racket was about." He glanced around his feet. Sawdust, nails, chunks of wood and an assortment of tools littered the floor.

She shrugged. "I needed another sawhorse."

As if that excused the last half hour of earsplitting noise. Her lack of remorse raised his level of irritation. "At nine-thirty at night?"

She laid her hammer down. "So?" Using both

hands, she brushed the sawdust off her jeans. "I'd like to be ready for tomorrow. I intend to get an early start."

Early? Keefe's eyes narrowed. Would he be up at the crack of dawn listening to power tools? He intended to disabuse her of that notion real quick. "How early?"

"Sometime after breakfast." Kitty unplugged her circular saw and wrapped the cord tightly around it. "Why? Am I bothering you?"

"You might say that."

"Well, I know of no way to muffle the sound of hammering, Dr. Brody. You might consider investing in a pair of earplugs. On second thought," she continued, giving him a sweet innocent look, "Just think how easy it'll be to keep tabs on me. When you hear hammering and sawing, you'll know I'm not slacking off." She turned and set her saw down near the wall. "It'll make supervising me that much easier."

Keefe chuckled softly. "My mother certainly got a bargain when she hired you, Miss O'Neill," he said, feeling a tug on his conscience when she turned and eyed him with wide-eyed naiveté.

"Oh? How so?"

He ignored the twinge of guilt. "You're a carpenter *and* a comedienne." He grinned, glad for the opportunity to zing one back at her. "Two for the price of one."

He watched as Kitty's face reddened. Direct hit. She opened her mouth to reply and probably would have stated her opinion of him loud and clear. But a movement at the doorway distracted them. Beth came into the room, looking rather stunned.

"I just got off the phone with Aunt Helen," she announced, her voice shaking. She combed her hands through her hair, leaving the brown strands sticking up in comical tufts. "We've got big problems."

Keefe had never seen his normally upbeat cousin in such distress. His heart thudded ominously. "What is it?"

"You'll never believe what she wants to do. I can't believe it myself." Beth rubbed her temples. Her eyes were wide with disbelief. "Oh, how could she!"

Keefe grabbed her by the shoulders, forcing her to look at him. "Tell me."

Beth stared up at him forbiddingly. "She must be angrier with you than I thought . . ." Her words trailed off and she jammed her hands at the waist of her blue chinos.

Keefe dropped his hands. "What has my mother done now?" It had to be something big to have Beth this upset.

"She wants to sell Lakeview Manor. She's put it on the market."

"What!" Keefe looked utterly shocked. "Mother would never—"

"It's true," Beth insisted. "That's why she's hired Kitty to fix the west wing. The realtor had suggested it to attract more buyers and command a better price. Apparently someone is already interested in buying it and the surrounding property. He wants immediate possession as soon as Kitty finishes her work." She gripped Keefe's arm, gazing up at him with a sense of urgency. "We have to change your mother's mind!"

Stunned, he stared at Beth, feeling like he'd just been punched in the stomach. "Who's the buyer?"

Beth hesitated for a brief second. "Wendell Burkett."

Keefe's eyes narrowed as he tried to place the name. He was sure he'd heard it before.

Beth arched a brow. "Let me refresh your memory. Remember that huge development of houses which went up near Ticonderoga five years ago?"

"Those tract houses." Now he remembered. A cold feeling seeped into his veins. "Wendell Burkett buys up large parcels of real estate and then develops the hell out of them." The seriousness of the situation suddenly became crystal clear. "If he can buy Lakeview Manor he'll bulldoze every acre to make room for those cheap houses."

Beth nodded solemnly. "Exactly."

Kitty felt her heart sink at the idea. Although she had no emotional investment in Lakeview Manor, she knew how devastating this bit of news was.

"Damn," Keefe growled. "I had no idea she wanted to sell the place." He raked back his hair, then rubbed the knot of tension at the back of his neck as an unwelcome feeling of fear snaked through him, tightening his muscles.

He couldn't believe his mother would do such a thing without consulting him.

He shut his eyes briefly but couldn't block out the images filling his mind. He could see the bulldozers now, cutting a swath through hills and century-old trees, wiping out woodland and wildlife habitats, and carving out new roads and driveways and parking lots. The thought sickened him.

"Lakeview Manor has been in the family for three generations." He faced Beth, giving her a hard look. "Why would she sell it?"

"She wants to live in Boca Raton year-round. She found a condo she likes, and—"

"But that's no reason to sell. She knows I'd stay here. What else did she say?"

"She said . . ." Beth paused and lowered her lashes, unable to look her cousin in the eye. "She said Lakeview Manor should be a family home. She's tired of waiting for you to settle down. She won't let you turn the house into a . . . bachelor pad."

"All because I stopped seeing Liz!"

"Liz, and the others." Beth folded her arms and looked at Keefe, her eyes daring him to argue. "Face it, Keefe. Your mother has a point. Your past relationships have been anything but steady. You've brought a constant stream of women in and out of Lakeview Manor. Don't deny it!"

"Maybe I like seeing a lot of women."

Kitty arched one slim brow, not caring for the sound of that statement. "Perhaps you'd like me to install a revolving door out front when I'm finished in here," she suggested pleasantly. "It'd be a great time-saver for you."

Beth threw back her head and laughed heartily. "Good one!"

Keefe glared at them both. "My relationships are

of no concern to you. Or my mother," he snapped.
"She has no idea what Wendell Burkett would do to
this place if he got his hands on it!" Keefe headed
to the door. "I'm calling her."

"Wait!" Beth hurried after him, grabbing his arm
before he could leave. "She said not to bother calling. She refuses to talk to you!" She darted a nervous
glance at Kitty. "Besides, I haven't told you everything. I came up with a plan to change her mind,
but I . . . I don't think you're going to like it."

"A plan?" Keefe's brows drew together in an omi-
nous scowl. He knew Beth could be quite dangerous
when given free rein. "What kind of plan?"

"Um . . . I sort of told your mother that you broke
up with Liz because you were in love with someone
else." She waited for Keefe's reaction. When none
was forthcoming, she took a deep breath and
plunged ahead. "And I told her that the manor
wouldn't be a bachelor pad because . . . well, because
you just became—engaged."

"Beth!" Kitty gasped. Out of all Beth's impulsive
acts, this outright lie clearly took the prize.

Keefe let out a harsh laugh. "You're right. I don't
like it."

"So I got carried away," Beth said, a defensive edge
to her voice. "I was only trying to get her to stop the
sale. I know how much Lakeview Manor means to
you!"

"We can't just make up a story that I'm engaged,
Beth," he said gently.

She blew out a long breath and released his arm.
"I'm sorry. I shouldn't have lied. It was stupid. I don't

know what I was thinking. I just wanted her to change her mind."

"And did she?"

"Not exactly. She's put a hold on the deal. Just until July, though. That's when she's flying back to New York. She wants to stay here for a couple days and . . . and meet your—fiancée."

Keefe groaned. "Oh, God . . ."

"But if your mother approves of her, she'll reconsider selling." Beth brightened with the possibility. "She said she would!"

Kitty had expected Keefe to react with anger. After all, his lack of a fiancée would be all too obvious when Mrs. Brody came home. But he chuckled softly and gazed down at his cousin with good-natured tolerance. "A wasted trip if there ever was one," he commented wryly. "You might as well call her back and tell her you made the whole thing up. You know Mother won't be amused to come home and find there never really *was* any fiancée. Unless I meet someone, fall in love, and propose marriage before July."

Kitty couldn't resist taking another jab at Keefe. "You could propose to this Liz person," she volunteered. "That would solve all your problems."

"Like hell." Keefe shot her a damning look. "For all Liz cares, Lakeview Manor could be sold tomorrow."

"It couldn't be Liz anyway," Beth remarked to Kitty. "I already told Aunt Helen he's marrying someone else."

"Oh?" Keefe looked at her with amused interest.

"And just who is the lovely lady that I'm engaged to marry? Does this figment of your imagination have a name?"

Beth smiled sheepishly as a guilty flush stained her cheeks. "I told her it was . . . Kitty O'Neill."

Three

"No way."

"Come on, Kit! Just listen for a minute," Beth pleaded urgently. "Hear me out."

"No." Kitty bent to pick up her hammer. She refused to hear any more. "Don't bother explaining. I know what you're going to say. And it won't work."

"It *will* work," Beth insisted. "I've thought it all out. All you have to do when Aunt Helen comes is pretend you're going to marry Keefe, and—"

"You want me to fool your aunt into believing I'm in love with your cousin." Kitty gave a small, humorless laugh at the absurdity of the idea. "That's impossible. You'd need an actress with the skills of Michelle Pfeiffer."

She peeked over at Keefe and caught him grinning. If she had wanted to insult him with that last remark, she hadn't succeeded. She turned her back on them and continued to put her tools away. The vagaries of Beth's mind might have been endearing before, but this time her friend had gone too far.

Kitty could empathize with their predicament. The home they had known and loved since childhood was about to be sold to a builder who had more interest in the development potential of the property than the grandeur of the estate. Acres of prime woodland would be razed, tradition and memories and family history all plowed under, making way for cookie-cutter tract houses. The designer in her balked at that thought.

But what Beth wanted her to do was ridiculous at best and unethical at worst. Lying to an elderly woman. My God!

Beth looked annoyed. "What's the big deal? It's only for two days. You wouldn't actually have to marry him!"

"You got that right." She gave Beth a long, hard look and then continued tidying up. She needed to concentrate on something else, forget Beth's wild scheme.

Forget, too, that Keefe was still watching her. He had said nothing for several moments. Would he consider taking part in Beth's hoax? Kitty wondered, despite her resolve not to explore the matter further, just how he'd play the charade if she had agreed to go along. Would he be attentive? Doting? Would he want to touch her? Kiss her?

She picked up her sawhorse and set it in the corner, trying to ignore the blast of heat that surged through her veins. She blamed it on the physical exertion of her work. Of course it wasn't due to the thought of the two of them acting like lovers.

"It'll be easy, Kitty," Beth insisted. "Just be nice to each other while Aunt Helen's here. Pretend you're deeply in love. She'll be fooled into thinking there's

going to be a marriage sometime in the future.
What's so hard about that?"

Kitty continued to ignore her.

Beth groaned in frustration and cast a desperate
look at her cousin. "You'll do it, won't you, Keefe?"

His broad shoulders moved in a careless shrug. "I
don't see how it can work, Beth. The charming and
lovely Miss O'Neill doesn't seem to like me."

Kitty ground her teeth at his sarcasm, then forced
a smile. "What's there to like?"

"I can think of a few things," he said, giving her
a suggestive grin in return. "Want to find out?"

"When pigs fly."

"You'd better watch out. Porky could be coming
in for a landing any time now."

Kitty contemplated bashing him one over the
head. Her eyes flashed as she picked up a wrench.
"Have I ever told you you're a remarkably charming
man?"

"No."

"Well, I'm not telling you now, either."

"You sure about that, sweetness?"

"Stop it, you two!" Beth's face was bright red with
anger. "You're both behaving like school children.
You've done nothing but snipe at each other. Can't
you try to get along? At least while Aunt Helen's
here?"

Keefe frowned at his cousin, annoyed. "I've got
better things to do with my time than play games,
Beth."

For a moment Beth looked indignant. Then a sly
expression stole over her face. "I see. So it's okay

with you when Wendell Burkett waltzes in and takes
over the manor. He'll live in this house and buy up
every last acre of property. He'll plow through the
woods and plant tacky little houses where hundred-
year-old evergreens grow . . ." She paused dramati-
cally. "Of course he'll probably tear down that old
tree house you built on Lookout Hill when you were
thirteen and replace it with some burger joint. Or a
mini mall," she added, the very idea making Keefe
wince. "All because you have better things to do with
your time. What in heaven's name could you have to
do that's more important than keeping Lakeview
Manor?"

Keefe glanced away and sighed heavily in defeat.
Beth had him there. The answer, of course, was nothing. Not even the historical biography he intended
to write held the same importance as keeping
Lakeview Manor. Beth's plan was a long shot, but
what other option did he have? If his mother was
mad enough to sell the manor, there was little chance
she'd back down.

He glanced over at Kitty. To say she didn't like him
was a huge understatement. It would take a lot of
work to convince his mother they were in love.

"All right. You've talked me into it," Keefe said.
"Your plan just might work. But there's no point in
even discussing it if Kitty is unwilling to participate."

Kitty whirled around and stared at him in disbelief.
He had sounded as crazy as Beth. "You'd actually go
along with this?" she challenged him. "You'd lie to
your mother?"

"To keep Lakeview Manor?" He looked down at

her with an expression that seemed to say she was being thickheaded. "Yeah. I guess I'd do almost anything. Even something as outlandish as pretending to be in love with you."

Keefe's remark stabbed at her. "Such a flattering way of putting it," she commented, trying her best to ignore the blow to her feminine pride.

"I figured you'd appreciate honesty."

"Honesty?" She raised one brow and looked at him. "Why bother? Beth's plan is one big lie. There's no honesty in pretending to be engaged."

"Touché, Miss O'Neill," he said with a slight bow. He grinned, noticing that her eyes had turned the same deep shade of blue as her jeans. Damn, but she was pretty when she was angry. He suspected that telling her that would only make her angrier.

He planned to tell her as soon as possible.

"Why won't you do it?" Beth asked, her voice trembling as she fought off tears. "Please, Kitty . . ." she whispered. "I don't know what I'd do if I couldn't come to Lakeview Manor anymore. Some of the happiest days of my life were spent here." She sniffed and wiped away a tear.

Kitty sighed, her heart aching for her friend. "Beth," she began gently. "It just doesn't seem . . . *right.* I couldn't lie about something as serious as marriage. And it wouldn't be fair to Mrs. Brody. Besides, think about it. The phony engagement couldn't go on forever. She'd only put the manor up for sale again when we called it off."

"No, she wouldn't!" Beth countered vehemently. "Not if you make it a long engagement. By then we'll have convinced her not to sell. I'm sure of it! All we need is time!"

Kitty felt a stab of remorse. The future of Lakeview Manor, the loveliest Victorian estate she had ever seen, rested squarely on her shoulders. And so did Beth's happiness. Kitty couldn't ignore the pleading look on her dear friend's face. Would Beth's scheme really be so bad? She'd only have to play Keefe's fiancée while Mrs. Brody visited. Two days. That was all.

"Come on, Kitty. Do it," Beth urged, her hands clasped in prayer. "Please."

Kitty glanced at her friend and her heart twisted. Beth was on the verge of tears again. How could she let her down when the manor meant so much to her? She had to help Beth. She owed her that much, at least. Beth had always been such a loyal friend. When Jay had broken her heart, it was Beth who had been there to pick up the pieces.

"Oh, all right," she muttered wearily, throwing caution to the wind. "I'll do it."

Beth gave a great sigh of relief. "Thanks, Kitty. You won't regret it!" She smiled brightly. "Congratulations! As of now, you two are officially engaged."

Beth's pronouncement made Kitty's stomach do a cartwheel. She peeked at Keefe and found him watching her, his eyes simmering with an unspoken challenge. She suddenly began to feel that she'd made a very poor decision.

"If only I had some champagne!" Beth moaned. "We could toast to your future. The future of Lakeview Manor, I mean," she amended quickly.

"There's time for that later," Keefe said. "I've got to get back to work." He strode to the door only to stop short. Before Kitty knew what to expect, he turned and came back, settling his hands on her waist. Dipping his head, he brushed his lips against the curve of her cheek, temptingly near the corner of her mouth.

Kitty blinked and backed away, her heart thundering. "What are you doing!"

"Kissing the bride to be." His teeth flashed in a seductive smile. "I can't wait for the honeymoon." After winking outrageously, he walked out the door and headed back to his study. Kitty stared after him, her emotions and her pulse in a state of turmoil. What was she getting herself into?

Beth giggled and clapped a hand over her mouth.

Kitty turned a withering stare her way. "I won't regret it, huh? You both think this is a joke!"

Beth apologized quickly. "This *is* a serious matter," she assured her. "But I think Keefe likes you. Honest."

"Gee . . ." Kitty's mouth twisted wryly. "How can you tell? The obnoxious behavior? The constant insults?"

"Those aren't insults," Beth said loftily. "It's flirting. And it's a side of Keefe I've never seen." She gave Kitty a big grin. "I think it's charming."

Kitty sighed as she picked up her toolbox and placed it near her sawhorse. It was obvious Keefe could do no wrong in his cousin's eyes. "It's late, Beth. Go to bed."

* * *

It was after eleven o'clock by the time Kitty stepped outside to retrieve her suitcases from her truck. Except for the wet driveway, glistening like a shiny black ribbon, all traces of the storm had vanished. A quarter moon slipped through a scattering of wispy clouds, and a handful of stars dotted the night sky. The air was fresh and clean, the tang of pine and the sweet scents of lilac and wisteria mingling into a fragrance as intoxicating as incense.

Quite a difference from Philadelphia, Kitty reflected in amusement, thinking of the combined aroma of cheese steaks with onions, freshly baked soft pretzels, and car exhaust that normally wafted up to the balcony of her city apartment.

She pulled her heaviest suitcase from the back of the truck, dropped it with a thud, and exhaled tiredly. The day had been physically and emotionally taxing.

"Let me help you with those."

Keefe's voice had startled her and she jerked around in surprise, saying nothing as he moved closer. He stopped less than a foot away, a solid shield between her and the star-flecked sky. Once again she felt overwhelmed, too aware of the size and strength of his body, the masculine sexuality that emanated from him like an aura. She fought to ignore the strange sense of arousal that came to life.

"Oh. It's you," she said without enthusiasm, turning back to her luggage.

He chuckled at her tone of voice. "Surprised?"

She yanked out another heavy bag. "Actually, yes, I am. I wasn't expecting you'd be supervising my every move."

"Who says I'm here to supervise?" he asked good-naturedly. "I came out to give you a hand."

She stared up at him over her shoulder, still wary, though her eyes sparked with sudden mischief. "If by a hand you mean a round of applause, then no thanks."

He let out another laugh. "Well, well . . . I was hoping I'd get to see that charming sense of humor again."

Scowling at that, she grabbed another bag.

He started to reach around her for the heavier suitcase. "I'll take this upstairs for you." His arm brushed her shoulder and she jumped at the touch, bumping her knee on the back of the truck.

"No!"

He looked down at her with mild amusement. "Why not?"

She glared at him, the throbbing in her knee making her temper rise. Why was he suddenly so solicitous? She knew he didn't want her here. Didn't approve of her for the renovation work. Didn't even like the noise she made. And Beth wanted them to pretend they were in *love?*

Beth was either crazy or hopelessly optimistic.

There were just too many conflicting emotions where Keefe Brody was concerned. He exasperated her. He made her angry. And yet . . . And yet she couldn't stop her pulse from leaping at the sight of him. Even his voice seemed to reach deep inside her, hum pleasantly through her whole body. And the simple, accidental touch of her shoulder a moment ago still had her flustered.

Her reaction made no sense.

"Look, it's nothing personal, but I don't need your help," she said finally. "I can manage by myself."

"I'm sure you can." Then he bent down and picked up the suitcase anyway, ignoring her protest. He held it easily in his hand, as if it were empty and not stuffed to capacity with Kitty's clothes. "But not this time."

She stared up at him, an indignant look on her face. This was one battle she apparently wasn't going to win. Heaving a sigh, she bent and picked up the other suitcase. He took that one from her hand as well, and his fingertips slid over hers for one long, slow moment. She jerked her hand away as if she had been burned.

"I said I could manage, Dr. Brody."

"Call me Keefe. There's no need for such formality, *Miss* O'Neill," he mocked. "We're engaged, after all."

"Only for the two days your mother is here," she quickly pointed out. "Until then, I'll be too busy to even think about Beth's scam."

"All work?" He tilted his head, and the moonlight gleamed in his eyes. "Even the most dedicated professional takes some time off for pleasure." He moved closer, his wide shoulders narrowing her world, blocking off the light on the porch. She edged back and bumped into her utility truck, suddenly afraid he might kiss her.

Smother her with kisses, was how Beth had put it.

Seconds stretched out endlessly as his eyes, dark with promise, fastened with frank appraisal on her mouth. "Don't you ever stop to have fun?" he murmured, his voice low and intimate, awakening every nerve ending in her flesh.

She shook off the instinctive arousal that pulsed in her veins. What was it about this man that caused such an effect? "Fun?" she asked, her lip curling. "I'm here to work. If I had wanted a vacation, I would have brought my bathing suit, not my tools."

Lifting her chin haughtily, she grabbed her handbag and the two smaller pieces of luggage, and went inside.

Keefe followed her upstairs to the guest room. "I see you've chosen the Forget-Me-Not room," he remarked. He stopped in the doorway and leaned against the frame.

"Beth chose it for me," Kitty replied abruptly, giving her surroundings a quick glance. The guest room had been named for the dainty blue forget-me-not wallpaper that covered the top half of the walls, above white paneling. White rattan furniture, pretty pastel hook rugs, and lacy curtains lent a romantic touch to the room.

Kitty set her bags down at the foot of the bed and tossed her purse on top. "Is that a problem?"

"Not at all," he said with a grin. "It's right across from mine. Pretty convenient, huh?"

She stared at him, feeling oddly breathless. This was too much. Beth was doing her best to make their pretend engagement as real as possible.

Keefe straightened away from the doorjamb and crossed over to the bed, setting her suitcases down. "If there's anything you need, you know where to find me."

She was still staring at him, feeling inexplicably shy. But his presence, so utterly masculine among the feminine décor of the room, seemed overwhelming. He stood by the bed, his hand resting on the rattan headboard, one denim-clad leg casually bent at the knee, brushing against the ruffles and flounces of the coverlet. The bed seemed soft and inviting. A place where a man and woman could spend the hours tangled in cool white sheets. . . .

Her pulse flared, quick and hot. She tore her gaze away, rattled by her provocative imagination. "Thank you," she managed, cursing the sudden tremor in her voice. She began to busy herself with her luggage, willing her hands to stop trembling.

"Goodnight, Kitty," he said after a moment, crossing to the door. "Sleep well."

She heard the soft click of the door as he left. Then, seconds later, the sound of another door closing directly across the hall. Giving up her pretense of unpacking, Kitty collapsed on top of the bed, exhaling as if she had been holding her breath all evening.

It was going to be a long summer.

"Most of this wainscoting is ruined," Beth pointed out the next morning.

Kitty poked her fingernail into the rotted wood at the base of the windows, chipping off flakes of white paint and leaving small dents in the spongy pine. "It's just surface damage," she commented. "I'll check the condition of the walls underneath when I remove the old paneling." Kitty hoped there wasn't any sign of water damage behind the wainscoting. Replastering the underlying walls would be costly and time-consuming.

She gave the perimeters of the solarium a quick scan to get a rough estimate on square footage. The room was large, taking up most of the west wing. Ringed on three sides with tall windows rising from hip level, it boasted an abundance of natural light. The ceiling rose two full stories. Four wide skylights on the southern slope of the roof opened at the touch of a switch. Morning sun beamed in, splashing golden light across the glazed brick floor.

Beth had pushed aside all the furnishings in the room to give Kitty better access to inspect the ruined paneling. The center of the room was a jumble of wrought iron chairs, glass-topped tables, and potted ficus and palm plants.

"These new windows cost Aunt Helen a small fortune," Beth explained. "They had to be custom-made the same size as the original ones." She opened a window. Cool air eased through the screen. The chirping and warbling of finches and wrens filled the room. Philadelphia, with its noise and commotion and stress, suddenly seemed a million miles away.

"Unfortunately," Beth continued, "by the time she found out the old windows leaked, the wainscoting had already been damaged beyond repair. The guy who installed the new windows offered to panel over the old wainscot with plastic veneer. Something in a faux wood grain. Can you imagine that?" She shuddered and gave Kitty a look of horror. "Plastic!"

"Now that goes against *my* grain." Kitty couldn't help snickering.

Beth groaned at the awful pun and shook her head. "That was bad, Kit." She grabbed her pencil and clipboard. "Come on. I'll help you take some measurements. Then we can make up an estimate for material."

Still grinning, Kitty unclipped the retractable tape measure from the waistband of her jeans and got busy. For the next hour they worked quietly, Beth jotting down numbers on a clipboard while Kitty measured. Kitty had never seen such a volume of woodwork. She'd need to order new paneling for the wainscot and custom trim for the windows and doorways. The existing ceiling crown looked to be salvageable, needing only a quick touch-up with paint.

She retracted her tape and clipped it back on her belt, making a mental note to add paint to the material list.

"Well, that's that." Beth stuck her pencil behind her ear. "You want to get another cup of coffee?"

"Sure." A shot of caffeine was just what Kitty needed. She'd had a restless night. Thoughts of Keefe, the pretend engagement, and even Jay Hilliard had whirled around and around, keeping her mind too active to sleep. Odd how the renovation work—the main reason she had come to upstate New York—had been the furthest thing from her mind.

She followed Beth into the kitchen and got two mugs out of the cupboard while her friend scooped coffee into the filter basket.

"I'm so glad you decided to help fool Aunt

Helen." Beth shot Kitty a grateful look as she filled the coffee maker with water and plugged it in. "Keefe's breakup with Liz was the last straw."

"Does he do that often? Break up with women, I mean." Apparently, the handsome professor had a serious problem with commitment.

Beth shrugged. "He's dated a lot of women, I guess. But he can't seem to find the right one. Before Liz, he dated Susan. Before Susan, there was Kara. She didn't last long at all. And before Kara, there was . . . oh, what *was* her name? Melissa? Melinda?"

"Never mind. I get the picture." The man obviously changed lovers as frequently as socks. Another modern-day Lothario. Just like Jay, Kitty thought disgustedly, vowing silently to steer clear of that type of man for the rest of her life.

"None of those women was right for him," Beth said crisply, rushing to his defense. "Especially Liz. But she lasted the longest out of all of them. Aunt Helen had hoped they'd get married. She's dying to have a fancy wedding here at the manor. But truthfully, I was glad when I heard they had stopped seeing each other."

"Why?" Kitty asked, curious despite herself. She told herself she couldn't care less about anything concerning Keefe Brody and his bevy of women, then waited to hear Beth's reply all the same.

Beth thought for a moment, then shrugged. "Because they're so different."

"Opposites are supposed to attract, Beth."

"Yeah, I know. But there still has to be some common ground. Something that makes them want to spend their lives together."

The coffee maker gurgled to a stop. Beth picked up the carafe and filled both mugs. As they sat at the table sipping the hot coffee, Beth expanded on the subject of Keefe's latest girlfriend.

"Liz prefers designer clothes and champagne and caviar and expensive nights on the town. But Keefe likes faded jeans, popcorn, and quiet walks by the lake."

Kitty blew on her coffee and took a tiny sip. "There must have been something that attracted them to each other," she commented absently.

"Yeah," Beth said with a smirk. "Sex."

"Beth!" Kitty looked around quickly, hoping the subject of their conversation wasn't listening in. Beth could be embarrassingly frank at times.

"Oh, don't worry!" She giggled at Kitty's panic-stricken face. "He's out on the lake, just like every morning when he's here. Unless it rains, of course. He paddles for a while, then comes back." She raised a brow at Kitty. "Where do you think he got such impressive biceps?"

"I hadn't noticed," Kitty said primly, taking a dainty sip of her coffee, trying to focus her mind on something else. *Paint. She had to remember to order lots of white paint.*

There was no fooling Beth. She laughed out loud. "Right."

Four

Kitty slipped the pry bar behind a section of wainscoting and gave it a sharp yank. Old rusty nails screeched in protest as the board splintered away from the wall, bits and pieces of rotted wood showering the floor at her feet. She ran her hand along the underlying wall. Both plaster and furring strips were dry, a good indication the damage was confined only to the surface woodwork.

Not having to repair the wall definitely made her job easier.

Moving to the next section, she felt along the side edge of the wainscoting, searching for a spot to fit her tool. She inserted it about midway down and gave it a few hard pulls. The panel clattered to the floor. She took a deep breath of satisfaction and pushed a strand of hair out of her eyes.

"Enjoying yourself?"

Kitty swung around, her left hand pressed to her heart, her pulse hitting the ceiling. Keefe stood at the doorway, leaning casually against the frame, arms folded across his chest. He was dressed in khaki shorts and a sun faded black T-shirt that looked as though it had been fashioned for a smaller man. The soft cotton hugged him like a second skin, outlining every muscle in his shoulders and biceps.

Devilish humor twinkled in his eyes as he watched her right hand tighten around the pry bar. "I hope you don't plan to use that thing on me."

"Only if you keep sneaking up on me," Kitty grumbled, angry that he had caught her off guard. He had scared the life out of her, just as he had done the moment they had met. "You have a habit of doing that. At least cough, or something."

"You want me to make more noise?" His teeth flashed at her. "You got it, sweetheart." He stepped outside the doorway, out of view, stamping and shuffling his feet with enough noise to rival a herd of elephants. When he finally reappeared, Kitty was laughing in spite of herself.

"How was that?" He was grinning as he walked over. "Loud enough for you?"

She nodded, her laughter subsiding into a warm smile. His noisy entrance had sounded ridiculous. She couldn't help but think he was nothing like the straitlaced and somber professors she had had in college. "For me and perhaps your closest neighbors."

He cocked his head, watching the transformation come over her. The bright smile illuminated her face, making her dark blue eyes sparkle like a starry midnight sky. Her teeth were pretty and straight and white as pearls, and a tiny dimple appeared at the right corner of her mouth. He felt as though the breath had been knocked out of him. And by something so simple as a genuine smile.

"You know, that's the first time you really smiled

at me," he said. "You should do it more often."
There was a slight pause while he leaned closer, mere
inches away from touching her. "It knocks me right
off my feet."

He was teasing, but there was something about the
way his gaze held hers that made her heart beat faster.
Kitty steeled herself against a sudden spark of desire.
"Then how come you're still standing?"

His deep laugh echoed in the solarium. "That's
what I like about you, Miss O'Neill. Your willingness
to put me in my place. No real wife could do a finer
job."

His eyes sparkled with boyish appeal. Kitty lowered
her gaze but found herself staring at his chest. Bad
move. "I've got work to do," she said a bit breathlessly. "Was there something you wanted?"

"Not particularly," he replied genially. "It's not
every day a part of Lakeview Manor gets torn down.
Do you mind if I hang around and watch?"

"I don't care what you do." That was a lie as big
as any she had ever told.

She adjusted the pry bar in her hand and turned
around, finding it impossible to ignore the tall man
standing so close behind her. His scent, woodsy and
clean, wrapped around her, and she found herself
gripping the tool tighter than she needed to.

Keefe's eyes swept the room while Kitty wrenched
off two more panels. He'd never really looked at the
condition of the solarium. He hadn't realized things
were so bad. This would be no quick spruce-up job.
The room had been neglected for years, and it
showed. The paneling beneath the windows had

warped and buckled from rainwater and excess humidity. The paint on the walls and ceiling was faded and peeling in spots. Much of the woodwork needed to be replaced. He wondered if one lone woman could tackle a job of this magnitude and do it right.

His gaze turned back to Kitty, sizing her up. He didn't think so.

"What do you do for jobs that require heavy lifting?"

She hesitated briefly then gave him a direct look. "I subcontract out the heavy work." A corner of her mouth lifted. "Big, strong men are a dime a dozen. No offense."

"None taken." He grinned at her attempt to insult him. He probably deserved it. But that didn't stop his questions. "That ladder you have strapped to your truck doesn't look tall enough to reach the ceiling." He watched as she struggled to remove another panel. She didn't appear inclined to reply to his comment. "How will you reach it?"

She pressed her weight into the pry bar and answered him on an intake of breath. "I'll rent scaffolding." She let out a gust of air as the panel finally popped off.

"After you've removed the old paneling, then what?"

"Then I replace it with new paneling." *Duh.* She rolled her eyes.

He frowned thoughtfully as he watched her work. "What about the windows?"

She stopped and straightened away from the wall,

wishing she could do her job without interruption. "What about them?"

"They need some sort of . . . wood around them."

"I realize that. It's called finish trim," she told him blandly.

"Have you ever done a window?"

"Of course I've done a window!" she responded, losing patience. Trimming out a window was probably one of the first things any carpenter learned. "What kind of a question is that?"

He shrugged. "I'm just curious."

She shook her head as she propped a hand on her hip. "It's more than just curiosity. You're checking up on me, aren't you?"

"Am I?" he asked mildly.

"Yes." Why else would he be eyeing her work and asking silly questions? "I know you've come to the conclusion that I'm not right for the job, but let me assure you I have never had a dissatisfied client. Just say the word and I'll give you a list of references." She lifted her chin and eyed him coolly. "Now, is there anything else on your mind, Professor Brody? Anything else you're wondering?"

His lips twitched slightly at her tone of voice. She had sounded like a stern teacher reprimanding a naughty pupil.

"Yeah." He leaned closer and his gaze settled on her mouth. "I'm wondering what it would be like to kiss you. A real kiss. On the lips."

Kitty's mouth opened in shock and her breath locked in her throat. He had said that intentionally to rattle her.

She gave him a look of disgust. "Why don't you just let me do my work!"

He held up his hands. "Who's stopping you?"

"You are," she countered through clenched teeth. "By distracting me with stupid questions and basically annoying me. Why?"

"Maybe I like to watch your eyes spark."

She counted to ten, and still felt angry. "You're wasting my time," she snapped. "The sooner I'm done, the sooner I'm out of here. Then we'll both be happy!"

"For heaven's sake, you two, stop arguing!" Beth said from the door. "I can hear you all the way down the hall."

"He started it." Kitty glared at him. "He's being a total pain in the—"

"Never mind who started it!" Beth said with visible annoyance. "You can't be arguing like this. You've got to start acting like you love each other. In fact, why don't you both take the rest of the day off and—"

Keefe held up a hand to cut her off and headed toward the door. "Not me. I've got too much work to do." And with that he left the room, leaving Beth scowling at his back.

"You two are either fighting or avoiding each other! We've got to start planning!" Beth pursed her lips, eager to get the charade under way. "What should we do first?"

"Order lumber and paint," Kitty suggested testily as she turned back to her work. That was her first priority, not her phony engagement to Keefe Brody. "I'm almost out of wood putty, too. Oh, and we'll need nails. Twenty-five pounds of casing nails, to start."

"That's not what I meant!" Beth said, the mundane subject annoying her. "We have to figure out how we're going to fool Aunt Helen. We can't just *tell* her you and Keefe are to be married. You have to show her you're right for each other so she approves of the engagement."

"How do you propose we do that?" Kitty asked. "We're not right for each other. We have nothing in common. We're complete opposites."

"You're the one who said opposites are supposed to attract!" Beth reminded her.

Kitty made a show of looking around the disordered solarium. "Look at this place, Beth! Right now I don't have the time to cultivate a relationship. Not even a fake one."

Beth groaned loudly. "Never mind about the renovation work for the moment," she demanded impatiently. "You and Keefe are more important. In order to pull this off, you have to spend more time with him."

"More time!" Kitty burst out, not liking that thought at all. "Isn't it enough I've agreed to 'marry' the man?"

"No." Beth frowned and became pensive. Then suddenly her face brightened and she grinned. "I know! How about dinner with him tonight?"

"Dinner?" Kitty passed the pry bar from one hand to the other, then back again as she considered the idea. They had to eat anyway. They'd find some place fast. In and out. One hour—two at the very most. "I suppose we could have dinner with him."

Beth snorted. "Who said anything about *we?*" She folded her arms and studied Kitty with a mischievous glint in her eyes. "I'm talking about you and Keefe. Alone. A quiet, candlelit restaurant. I'll make the reservations. I have just the place in mind."

Alone. She should have seen it coming. "I don't see what any dinner is going to accomplish," Kitty replied peevishly. Other than provide Keefe with another golden opportunity to belittle her with his opinions.

Beth sighed. "It'll accomplish a lot. You'll learn intimate little things about each other that all engaged couples should know."

"Intimate things?" Kitty gaped at her in alarm, then shook her head decisively. "Forget it. I know all I need to know about him right now."

"Oh, you do, do you?" Beth tilted her head to the side as she considered her friend. "When's his birthday?"

Kitty fiddled with the pry bar in her hand, dodging Beth's gaze. "I . . . uh . . . don't know," she mumbled.

"It's March twenty-sixth. Where does he teach?"
Silence.

"As his fiancée, you ought to know the location of his town house. Where is it?"

Kitty cleared her throat and shuffled her boots on the dusty floor.

"What does he like to do in his spare time?"

"Aha!" Kitty answered, raising one small fist in smug triumph. "I know that one! He likes to canoe!"

"So you got one out of four." Beth shook her head slowly, looking dejected. "I can see Aunt Helen will be fooled for about two seconds."

Kitty let out her breath and sat down wearily on the ledge of the open window, acknowledging the sudden butterflies in the pit of her stomach. "It's not going to work, is it?" she asked, realizing for the first time the difficult role ahead of her. She'd never convince Mrs. Brody she was in love with her son if she didn't know even the most basic things about him. "So what do I do?"

"Find out all you can about him. Even stupid little things like his favorite color, the music he likes, the size of his shirts, whether he sleeps in pajamas or not—"

"That's so personal!" Kitty sounded scandalized at the idea. "I could never ask him that! He might think that I—well, *think* about such things." She could almost see that slow lift of his eyebrow now.

"But do you see what I'm getting at?" Beth persisted. "The more you know about Keefe, the more believable you'll be as a couple in love." She fixed Kitty with a sly look. "Keefe will have to know some personal things about you as well."

Kitty clenched her teeth. This was all getting more complicated and more involved than she wanted it to. "Tell him my favorite color is blue," she said in a clipped voice as she rose to her feet and moved down to the next section of old paneling. "But whether or not I wear pajamas is something he'll *never* find out."

"Never is a long time," Beth said with a laugh as she headed to the door. "But tonight you can tell him anything you want. How about reservations for eight o'clock?"

"Oh, all right!" Kitty relented. "But this isn't a dinner date. I'm only going out with him to ask questions!"

"Whatever!" Beth called gaily.

Kitty watched her friend walk away, wishing every restaurant in Lake George was booked solid for the night.

The idea of Wendell Burkett owning Lakeview Manor appalled Harold Sugarman. After forty years as caretaker of the Victorian estate, every tree on the property was as dear to him as an old friend.

He jabbed his trowel disgustedly into the bed of topsoil and proceeded to work a small section loose, muttering and complaining under his breath.

Keefe bent down and handed him another impatiens, watching as the old man deftly sank the tiny starter plant into the rich loam. He could tell Hal was upset. He could also count on him to help in any way possible.

"Mother is due to visit in July, Hal. I'll need you to act like Kitty and I are engaged. Pretend it's nothing out of the ordinary . . ."

"As far as I'm concerned, sir, I'm hearing wedding bells already." Harold sat back on his heels, brushing the dirt from his hands as he glanced up at his boss. "I can't imagine what got into Mrs. Brody to try to sell this place!" He shook his head, still astonished that the grounds he had so lovingly tended for so many years were in jeopardy. "I hope Beth's plan works."

That was the predominant thought in Keefe's mind hours later as he tried without success to get some work done. He leaned back in his chair and stared at the half-empty computer screen. The thin black cursor flashed at him, demanding further input. Blink. Blink. Blink.

It was no use. He couldn't concentrate.

Letting out his breath in irritation, he punched in the command to save his file. Then he pushed himself away from his desk to look out the trio of windows behind him.

It was nearly five-thirty. The afternoon sun filtered through the oak and spruce trees standing sentinel around the manor. Patches of cool shade dappled the side yard. Harold's green-thumb touch was apparent everywhere—in the weedless lawn, in the glossy foliage of the periwinkle edging the woods, in the precision-trimmed hedges of yew and boxwood.

Keefe regretted having worried Hal. The old caretaker took an immense amount of pride in his work. That it could all be bulldozed away had not been welcome news.

Keefe couldn't let that happen. Lakeview Manor was his refuge. There was never a time he didn't come here and feel a profound peace—a peace that all too frequently eluded him at his city town house. He doubted there was anyone else who felt that same measure of serenity here.

Keefe turned away from the window as if in pain. His mother's plan to sell Lakeview Manor was a betrayal that cut deep. She knew how much the estate meant to him. But she put it on the market anyway, attracting the likes of Wendell Burkett, a man who wouldn't merely own the property, but destroy it as well.

Now he was forced to lie to his mother. And lying never sat well with him. But what else could he do? Playacting the role of husband-to-be was his only chance. If he and Kitty played everything just right, his mother would head back to Florida, happy that her son had finally settled down with the right woman.

Big if.

Kitty glanced at her watch again. Seven-forty. She sighed and checked her appearance in the mirror on the foyer wall, trying to ignore the butterflies fluttering in her stomach.

What was there to be nervous about? Just because she hadn't been on a date in years . . .

But this was *not* a date. It was a simple dinner appointment. Nothing more. Beth had made such a big deal about it, though, encouraging her to wear one of the two dresses she had thrown in her suitcase at the last minute before leaving Philadelphia. Tonight she had chosen the simple chemise-style dress, an elegant garment in peacock-blue silk, tailored with discreet tucks at the waistline to enhance the slim curves of her figure.

Kitty bit her lip as she gazed with a critical eye at her reflection. Gently she smoothed a hand over her hair, making sure all the pins securing her French twist were in place. She straightened the cuff of her sleeve, fussed at the delicate gold chain around her neck, then checked the hem of her dress.

"You look gorgeous!" Beth assured her, bustling into the foyer. "And aren't you glad I made you pack that dress? That shade of blue is perfect on you. It's nice to see you wearing a dress for a change. And heels, too."

Kitty wrinkled her nose. "I'm not comfortable in the least," she complained as she flexed her right foot. "I'll probably trip over something and fall flat on my face."

"That won't happen." Beth's smile brimmed with impish delight. "Keefe is so gallant, he'll catch you before you hit the ground."

Kitty caught her friend's eye in the mirror. Beth's remark had thrown her, bringing back a vivid memory of Keefe carrying her into the study.

Slightly shaken, she moved away from the mirror and took a deep breath as she began to pace the foyer. "Isn't it time to go?" She wanted to get this over with.

"Keefe will be out front any second. He's getting his Jeep out of the garage now." Beth pushed aside the curtain and peeked out at the driveway. "Remember what I told you, Kitty. Ask a lot of questions. Find out everything you can about him."

"Do you have a pen?"

Beth turned away from the window, frowning. "What for?"

"So I can take notes." Kitty's smile was saccharine sweet.

"Very funny."

They both turned at the sound of the Jeep's motor. "Let him come in here for you," Beth said, stopping Kitty before she could head out the door.

"I prefer to think of this as a business meeting, Beth." Kitty resumed her pacing. "This isn't some formal romantic date, you know. I could meet him out front."

Hell, she could meet him over the kitchen table, ask a few questions, jot down some notes, and be on her way. That would have accomplished the same thing. No sense bringing dinner into it. But Beth wouldn't have it.

The oak door swung open and Keefe was there. His eyes met Kitty's. Her heart slammed in her chest and she nearly bumped into the credenza. He looked stunningly handsome, a pale gray linen suit accentuating his powerful build to masculine perfection. A crisp white shirt and black silk tie complemented his rugged dark looks. The setting sun beyond the door framed him in golden light, emphasizing his height and the strength in his broad shoulders, gleaming on the coal-black strands of his hair. Despite the civilized clothes, there was an element of untamed power about him that raised Kitty's pulse. She put a hand on the edge of the credenza to steady herself.

Keefe stared back at Kitty, his gaze taking in every detail of her appearance. To see how perfectly she had transformed from a denim-clad carpenter into an elegant, polished woman didn't surprise him. He had known from his first glimpse of her that she was beautiful.

What did surprise him was his reaction. He felt as though he had been hit with a shock wave.

"You look lovely," he murmured in a low, husky voice that curled around her, tingling every inch of her flesh. He stood back from the door to let her pass. "Ready to go?"

"Of course," she answered, struggling to keep her voice light and carefree.

A business meeting, she told herself again. *That's all this is.* She edged past him, feeling his eyes follow her as she walked down the steps to the dark green Cherokee idling quietly in the driveway.

Keefe was beside her in an instant, opening the car door for her. Despite her three-inch heels he still towered over her, and she was disturbed to find her legs suddenly feeling weak and unsteady. Good Lord, but she hadn't worn heels in years. She'd never get through the evening without stumbling.

She climbed into the Cherokee and adjusted her seat belt as Keefe took his place behind the wheel.

This is feeling more and more like a bona fide date, Kitty thought, breathing an audible sigh as Beth waved them off like a proud mother hen from the top of the steps.

Keefe leaned toward her. "Second thoughts?"

"Uh . . . no," she answered hesitantly, glancing at him. The space inside the Jeep seemed to shrink. She noted the swell of his shoulder, the controlled strength of his hands as he slid the stick shift smoothly into first and set the Jeep in motion.

Her tentative answer made him laugh. "You're sure about that?" He turned north onto Lake Shore Drive.

Kitty sighed again. "Dinner is so unnecessary," she insisted, gazing out the window at the passing scenery. What a ridiculous situation they were in! Forced to date each other to save the manor. She turned to look at him. "This is all Beth's idea, you know."

"Really," he commented dryly, keeping his eyes on the road. "And here I was hoping you were trying to get me alone so you could have your way with me."

He grinned at her, his teeth as bright as his snowy white shirt. His eyes were filled with such wicked humor her heart skipped a beat.

His gentle teasing showed her how silly she was being. She was making too big a deal out of this one dinner. All they had to do was spend time together. Get to know each other a little better. So what if she didn't like Keefe Brody? She could ignore his arrogance, his chauvinistic opinions, the compelling masculinity that seemed, oddly enough, to sap every ounce of her strength and control. She could pretend she liked him when Mrs. Brody was around. What could be simpler?

Perhaps solving the great mystery of life, Kitty

thought with wry humor. Nothing about Keefe Brody would be simple. She knew that.

She turned her head and concentrated on the fast-moving blur of pines as they drove in silence along the shadowy road.

Five

The Adirondack Inn was a rambling log and stone structure set on a gentle hill near the cool blue waters of Lake George. Despite its old logging-camp motif, the rustic inn was one of the more elegant dining establishments in the Lake George area, and one of the few that drew a regular crowd even during the off season.

Entering through the wide oak doors, they followed the maitre d' to a secluded, candlelit table with a view of the lake. Kitty opened her menu and scanned it quickly. Nothing appealed to her. She wasn't very hungry.

When the waiter arrived to take their orders, she chose the pasta primavera, the lightest entrée on the menu. She would make this evening as short as possible. A simple meal and a few questions. No coffee, no dessert.

Keefe ordered a shrimp appetizer with his prime rib dinner, and selected a bottle of merlot.

While they waited for dinner, Kitty decided to get the evening underway. She would learn all she needed to know during this one 'date.' When Mrs. Brody arrived in July, she would toss out a few pertinent details to prove she knew Keefe, and then smile sweetly and gaze at him with just the right amount of feigned adoration. Mrs. Brody couldn't help but fall for it.

"Beth said you teach history," she began, using her most businesslike voice. "Where do you teach?"

"The State University of New York," he answered, "at Albany." He took a slice of warm bread from the basket on the table and bit into it.

"How long . . . ?" Her question trailed away as her mind wandered to consider other things—the strong line of his jaw and the way the dancing flame of the candle flickered shadows across the angles of his face.

"How long what?"

Kitty blinked, snapping back to the present as the waiter arrived with Keefe's appetizer and the bottle of wine. She paused while he poured them each a glass. "How long have you been teaching?"

He shrugged and took a sip of his wine. "A few years."

"A few years?" she echoed. As his 'fiancée' she had to know exact answers. "Could you be more specific?"

"Five years," he said, then speared a tiny pink shrimp with his fork.

Five years, she repeated to herself, committing it to memory. She took a small sip of her wine and planned her next question. "Did you go to college there, too?"

"No." He seemed intent on enjoying his food, paying little heed to Kitty's questions. "Here," he said, reaching over the table with a forkful of shrimp. "I

order this every time I come here. The chef mari-
nates it in the most delicious sauce. Try it."

"No, thank you," she declined politely, eager to
get back to her questions. Beth had wanted her to
learn things of both a personal and professional nature. She had a lot of ground to cover. "Now then,
about your education—"

"You don't like shrimp?"

"Well, yes, as a matter of fact I do, but—"

"Taste it." He moved the fork closer to her mouth.

She sighed and gave in to his persistence, taking a
bite of the shrimp.

Keefe's eyes darkened as her lips closed around
the fork. He watched with rapt attention as she
chewed the tender mouthful and sighed in apprecia-
tion. When she licked the marinade from her bottom
lip, a blast of heat seared through his veins. For a
moment he had an overwhelming urge to shove the
small table aside and taste the marinade on her lips.

Good Lord, he must be crazy. He could well imagine her reaction to *that*.

"It's very good," she admitted. She paused for a
quick sip of wine. "Now, where was I? Oh, yes . . .
you said you didn't go to college in New York. Where
did you go?"

"Dartmouth."

"And your doctorate is in history, I assume," she
said, thinking aloud. "Were you in a fraternity?"

"No."

The waiter set their salads down. Kitty added a dol-
lop of dressing, then ignored her salad as she thought

of another question. "Did you always want to teach history?"

"No," he replied solemnly. "I wanted to be a cowboy."

She stared at him. "Be serious. This is important."

"So is dinner." He nodded to indicate her untouched salad. "Let's see if you can use that mouth for something other than talking." He held her gaze for a long, charged moment, then purposely lowered his eyes to her lips.

Kitty's face flamed at the image that leapt to mind. Her heart going like a jackhammer, she stabbed at a cucumber slice, more than happy to concentrate on her salad. It wasn't until she had polished off the last shred of romaine that she recovered her equilibrium.

But as soon as dinner arrived, she was ready with more questions. "What else do you do in your spare time besides canoe across the lake?"

"I canoe back."

She laughed at that, finding him amusing. But he didn't answer her question. "Come on, you must have some other hobby. Do you like to travel?"

Keefe hesitated, a forkful of baked potato midway to his lips. A look of mild irritation passed over his face. "Only if I have to."

"Do you like sports? What about music? Do you like opera? Classical? Or maybe you're a Top 40 kind of guy."

He chuckled softly at the rapid-fire questions and shook his head in amazement. She was as relentless as a reporter trying to meet a tough deadline. For a while he stared out at the lake, letting the silence stretch out between them, his eyes following the progress of a pleasure cruiser slowly making its way back to dock.

"Keefe?" She tilted her head and gazed at him with an expectant expression.

He turned back to look at her, feeling a jolt of something hot and vital course through him. Candlelight glittered in her hair, and danced and shimmered against the fabric of her dress. He wondered if she knew just how perfectly the blue silk brought out the color of her eyes.

He shook himself out of his reverie, irritated that she had cast such a strange spell over him. What the hell had happened to him? He was supposed to pretend he was attracted to her, not actually *be* smitten. He had no more control over his libido than one of his students.

Kitty frowned, growing uneasy by his expression. There was something in his eyes—a predatory, sexual look that hadn't been there before—and she shifted nervously in her seat. "I . . . I asked you about sports. And music."

"When are you going to stop this inquisition?" He bit into a piece of steak, chewed it thoroughly, then washed it down with the rest of his wine. "You've managed to turn what would have been a lovely dinner into a game of Twenty Questions. Why the in-depth interview?"

"Perhaps I've been a little intrusive," she conceded. "But we don't have time for . . . for lovely dinners if we want to get to know each other enough to fool—"

"Is that what this evening is all about?" he asked softly. "A crash course in Keefe Brody?"

"Yes, of course," she answered. "Why else am I here?"

"I see." Why had he thought otherwise? He had come for a nice evening out. Something he had actually looked forward to. She was only here to gather data. And that bothered him more than he'd like to admit.

God, he felt like a fool, getting all caught up in the idea of a damn date.

"Well, then, Kitty," he said conversationally. "So the evening won't be a total waste, I'll tell you all about myself." He paused to pour more wine. "I like fine wine and good Italian food. I like starry skies, moonlit boat rides on the lake. Sunny, lazy strolls through the woods. The crunch of leaves underfoot in the autumn. I like kids and puppies and Saturday matinees. Am I going too fast?"

Kitty blinked. "Uh . . . no."

"Good. You asked about sports. I guess football is my favorite." He leaned forward, his voice becoming more intimate. "Nothing beats a crackling fire on a rainy night or those low, bluesy notes of a jazz saxophone . . ."

Kitty leaned forward too, drawn in by his soft words, mesmerized by the husky depth of his voice.

"I prefer a comfortable pair of faded, well-worn blue jeans over a suit and tie any day of the week." He smoothed his hand over his black silk tie. "But I'm always happy to make an exception when I'm with a beautiful woman."

And there had to have been quite a few. Kitty couldn't stop the swift stab of jealousy as she pictured other women sitting in her place, laughing, flirting with Keefe, kissing him. . . .

She shook the image off impatiently. What was wrong with her! She had no right to jealousy—or anything remotely like it. Not in a pretend relationship.

"Have I satisfied your curiosity, Kitty?"

She hesitated, trying to think of other topics that hadn't been covered yet. "Your job—do you like it?"

He took a sip of wine, then picked up his fork again. "I find it very gratifying."

She waited for him to elaborate, but his attention was focused on his meal. "Gratifying in what way?" she prodded.

"When I've ignited a spark of interest in my class, when a struggling freshman finally aces a test, when I've made a dull period in history come alive for a student who once didn't give a damn."

He was giving her a lot of information she could use. Beth would be impressed. Kitty almost wished she had brought a pen to write it all down. "Anything else?"

The subtle change in his expression should have warned Kitty off. "You don't want to know any more."

"Of course I do," she assured him quickly, though her heart gave a serious thump. She could be stepping into dangerous territory. "If we're to play our parts right, we shouldn't keep secrets from each other."

He took a sip of wine, his eyes like hot embers as

he watched her over the rim of his glass. "All right. There is one subject we haven't gone over."

Kitty swallowed against a knot of apprehension, her throat dry. "What is it?"

"A secret." He put his glass down and leaned in closer. "Something I've kept to myself all night long."

Kitty's breathing went still. "Tell me."

His gaze drifted over her face, down the slender column of her throat and back to her upswept hair. "When you wear your hair up like that, all I want to do is press my lips into that enticing hollow just below your ear."

Kitty's hand flew to her throat as she gasped softly, shock and anger and fright all clashing like cymbals inside her. Whatever she had expected him to reveal about himself, that wasn't it.

"I suppose I deserved that," she said tightly. "Ask a lot of questions and you might get an answer you don't want to hear." She gathered up her purse to leave.

"Don't go." Keefe reached across the table and caught her wrist in a light grip as she started to rise. "I haven't asked my questions yet."

But instead of asking them, he picked up his fork and resumed eating as though nothing out of the ordinary had happened between them.

"Well?" she prodded after several minutes. She jiggled her foot and glanced at her watch. She was anxious to end the evening before he divulged any more of his so-called secrets.

Finally, he pushed his plate aside and settled back in his chair, his long legs stretched out lazily. "Beth tells me you're divorced. Why don't we talk about that?"

"There's nothing to say. We . . . it just didn't work out." That was a nice capsule summary of her marriage.

"How long were you married to Mr. O'Neill?"

"Two years. And his last name was Hilliard. O'Neill is my maiden name. I went back to it after Jay and I divorced." She glanced at the window on her right, keeping her eyes fixed on the flickering reflection of their candle. Thinking of those two years made her sigh heavily.

Keefe frowned at her pensive expression. "You look like you regret the divorce," he stated flatly. "Perhaps you still love him."

"No!" She turned to face him, astounded that he should think that. "And don't ask any more questions about him. There's no reason for you to know about my relationship with my ex-husband. It's past history."

"All the more reason to talk about it," he replied evenly. "Don't you know our pasts shape who we are?" He smiled and leaned forward, bracing both forearms on the table. "I can't think of a better way to get to know you than to delve into your past."

"This, from a history professor," she said, rolling her eyes. "What a surprise."

He laughed in genuine amusement. "Then may I proceed with my questions?"

"You may not," she said sternly, trying not to notice that when he laughed his eyes danced like green flames in the candlelight. "Pick another topic."

"Okay. How did you acquire so many debts?"

Her eyes narrowed at the personal question. "None of your business," she replied coolly.

"Why? Are your money problems tied in to your ex-husband?" He leaned closer and smiled. "Don't tell me you piled up those debts trying to buy his love. Or maybe it's because you never met a credit card you didn't like."

What little patience she had left vanished and she rose to her feet, clutching her purse with a white-knuckled grip. How could he joke about something that had caused her such financial difficulties and emotional turmoil? For a moment she didn't know who she was angrier with: Jay, for placing her in such straits, herself, for her own gullible naiveté, or Keefe, for making light of it.

"I think we both have all the information we need for one evening." She opened her purse and fumbled inside, grabbing some bills out of her wallet to pay for her dinner. She placed them on the table. "I'll be in the car."

She didn't wait for his response but rushed in a clatter of high heels out of the restaurant.

She didn't stumble once.

"I've ordered everything we'll need to finish the solarium," Beth cheerily informed Kitty. "And they'll deliver it all on Monday."

Other than a mumbled word of thanks, Kitty continued working in silence, stacking the old pine panels she had pried from the walls into neat piles for later removal. Then she picked up a broom and began sweeping the sawdust powdering the floor. She wanted to keep busy. Anything to keep her mind off last night. The dinner conversation had been bad enough; the silent drive home even worse.

Beth eyed her friend, a grim look clouding her dark eyes. "Last night's dinner must have been a disaster. You've been avoiding Keefe all day."

That remark merited Kitty's full attention. "Who says I'm avoiding him?"

"It's obvious you are," Beth countered. "You've worked nonstop for the past few hours. It's Saturday, Kitty. You can knock off a little early."

Kitty gave an exasperated laugh. "And do what?"

Beth shrugged and moved over to the window. The sound of a lawn mower drew her attention to the far edge of the yard. "Go for a walk in the woods," she suggested absently, her eyes following Harold Sugarman as he cut the grass in neat vertical rows. "Go down to the lake and relax on the dock. And when Keefe gets back from town—"

"No thanks." Kitty resumed sweeping.

"Have dinner with him again, Kitty," Beth pleaded, turning around. "Once isn't enough to get to know him."

"I think I know enough." *And then some.* "Mrs. Brody won't be here until July. I won't need to spend any more time with Keefe until then."

Beth's face fell. "You're going to just ignore him until Aunt Helen comes?"

"Yes. Why bother with the charade if she's not here to appreciate it? Don't worry, I'll put on a good show when she arrives." Kitty stopped to pick up a small scrap of lumber and toss it aside.

"You don't know him well enough to put on a good show."

"Fine. Tonight you can fill me in on any important details."

"I can't," Beth said simply. "I'm going out."

"You have a date?" Kitty pivoted in time to see a rare blush bloom over Beth's cheeks.

"Oh, Kitty, it's almost like it was meant to be! I mean, there I was in Glens Falls ordering lumber and paint, and guess who was behind the counter? Tom Jeffries!" she rushed on. "We went steady in high school. He owns the building supply store now." Beth clasped her hands beneath her chin and sighed dreamily.

"He asked me out to dinner."

Kitty smiled, thrilled for her romantic friend. "What time is he picking you up?"

"Six." She ran a hand through her hair and grimaced. "What time is it now?"

Kitty consulted her watch. "Four-thirty-five."

Beth gasped in a panic. "Little more than an hour to get ready. I've got to shower. And look at my hair! I'll need styling mousse. And a blow dryer. I'll need every minute!"

"You'd better go then!" Kitty chuckled as she shooed Beth out the door.

She was still smiling at her friend's nervous excitement as she resumed sweeping. It had been a long time since she had seen Beth this enthused about a date.

For the next hour, she organized her tools and cleared a spot in the corner for Monday's shipment of material. Finally, she had to stop as a big yawn overtook her. The long workday and lack of sufficient sleep from the night before had caught up with her, leaving her feeling dead on her feet. She needed some fresh air.

She stepped outside onto the patio and paused for a moment, face upturned to the afternoon sunshine. The air was warm, scented with spring flowers and newly mown grass. She stretched slowly, easing some of the tightness from her neck and shoulders.

Feeling rejuvenated, she headed toward the stone steps leading down to the lawn. And stopped, skin prickling at the back of her neck.

She knew instantly she wasn't alone.

Kitty turned slowly and gasped in surprise, unable to believe her eyes. Stretched out lazily in the corner of the patio, watching her every move from behind a pair of aviator sunglasses, was a man she had hoped she'd never see again.

She stared at her ex-husband, a mixture of dread and shock washing over her like ice water. He had found her. She had thought she was safe, but he was here. "Jay."

"I've been watching you through the window for the last half-hour," he said, grinning as if they were old friends. He rose from the chaise lounge and strolled across the patio as though he had every right to be there. "Still working as hard as ever, I see."

Kitty narrowed her eyes. She didn't trust the mega-watt smile Jay threw her way. "How did you find me?"

"Your landlord told me where you were. He didn't want to, at first. Until I said I needed to forward your alimony checks." He laughed at how easy it had been.

"Alimony!" Anger warmed the chill from her veins. "What alimony?" She'd received no money from Jay after their divorce, hadn't asked for anything at all from him. She'd simply wanted to be left alone. "Why are you here?"

"I wanted to see you." His smile disappeared in a flash. "We need to talk."

She stared at her ex-husband, thinking how little he had changed. He was still the Jay she remembered. Still dressed expensively, his clothes tailor-made to enhance his athletic physique. His light brown hair was salon styled, a few blond highlights streaked in for effect. He looked fit and tanned, like a successful businessman who spent his weekends on the golf course. But Kitty knew his healthy glow was due more to faithful tanning-parlor visits than actual time spent outdoors. Jay had always gone for fast, easy results.

"We have nothing to say to each other," she said finally. "I want you to leave."

He looked at her speculatively, then walked to the end of the patio. With an air of contentment about him, he sat down on a stone bench, giving his surroundings a critical eye before bestowing another smile on her.

She followed him. "I mean it, Jay. I want you to go."

"Lakeview Manor, huh? Very nice." His gaze took in the entire house from wing to wing. "This place must be worth a small fortune. They paying you well?"

Kitty wouldn't answer that. Or waste her time on small talk. The conversation already made her uneasy. Whatever reason Jay had for tracking her down all the way in Lake George couldn't possibly be good. She knew him too well.

"What do you want?" Her tone was cold.

"Is that any way to talk to an old friend?"

"We were married once, Jay. That doesn't entitle us to a lifelong friendship."

He shrugged and settled back on the bench, one arm draped comfortably along the top. "I need a favor."

There was only one thing Jay always needed. "How much?"

"Three thousand dollars."

"Three thousand—!" Kitty burst out incredulously. But she didn't know why she was surprised. Jay was simply being Jay. "No."

"Don't be so hasty," he cautioned softly. His eyes flashed behind the dark glasses. "Think it over. I'll pay you back."

"I've heard that before. And I don't have to think it over. The answer is still no." She folded her arms and frowned. "What do you need three thousand dollars for?"

"I owe someone some money."

"A bookie, you mean." Jay had wasted more money trying to get rich quick. He had always believed a fortune was as close as the next winning bet. Trouble was, Jay rarely won any amount substantial enough to offset his losses. "I'm right, aren't I? A bookie. Or a loan shark."

He didn't answer immediately, but glanced off toward the lake where cool water glittered brightly through a screen of white pine and balsam fir. He didn't appear troubled by her refusal, and Kitty wondered what else he had up his sleeve.

Finally, he looked at her and sighed. "You don't need to know who I owe it to."

"That's true. It doesn't matter. Because I can't give you three thousand dollars. I don't have it."

He laughed softly. "You're lying."

"Despite what you may believe, Jay, I don't have an endless supply of money. You can't just show up every time you're in a bind and demand cash."

He gave her another sunny grin. "I'm easy to please. I'll take a check."

"You'll take nothing." She turned to go.

He was on his feet in an instant, moving between her and the house. "You've got the money in your business account." He stared down at her, all traces of good humor gone. "Don't tell me a place like this is stingy with its funding. They've probably paid you a good percentage up front, haven't they? Hell, I could have asked for twice the amount and you'd have no problem coming up with it."

"If I could come up with ten times the amount, I still wouldn't give it to you. We're through, Jay. Remember? The divorce was final months ago. Find someone else to give you the money."

"All right," he agreed smoothly. "I'm sure your fiancé has plenty of cash." He was smirking now. "Maybe I'll go ask him for some."

Six

Kitty stared at the gloating expression on her ex-husband's face. Despite the heat of the afternoon sun, she shivered. "What?"

"Your fiancé. Or maybe I should say, your pretend fiancé." Jay removed his sunglasses and nibbled on the earpiece, his gray eyes amused. "And don't act so innocent. I know the whole plan." His gaze drifted over her. "Quite the little scam artist you've become, Kit. I like it."

Kitty's mind whirled. Jay *knew*. "Who told you?"

He shrugged lazily. "Some old guy mowing the lawn. Harold something. I told him I was your long-lost brother."

Kitty gasped at the lie. "I don't have a brother."

Jay hunched his shoulders. "So? He doesn't know that. All he knows is how much you've missed me . . ."

Kitty listened to him with growing anger, hating the smug grin plastered on his face. This was Jay as he had always been. He would do anything to get what he wanted. She had never known anyone so completely without morals.

"All I had to do was help him fill the mower with

gas, tell him what a nice job he was doing, basically act interested in the old guy. He was more than happy to chat the afternoon away. Anything you want to know about crabgrass, or Professor Brody, or phony engagements—Harold's the one to go to."

She stared at him with cold hostility. He had conned an old man, taken advantage of Harold's sweet, trusting nature. "I'm through bailing you out of trouble, Jay. I've given you enough money. You got half the equity in the sale of the town house—"

"And I could have tripled it if that stupid nag hadn't stumbled at the finish line!"

Kitty gaped at him. "You bet that money on a *horse?*"

"It was a sure thing!" His jaw worked furiously as his inner tension rose to the surface. Impatiently, he batted at the branch of an arborvitae. "I had an inside tip."

Kitty shook her head. "You'll never change, Jay. How much money have you thrown away like this over the years?"

"I didn't come here for a lecture, Kit." He flicked a bit of lint off his shirtsleeve, looking bored. "I came here for three thousand dollars."

"Then you came for nothing."

"You're refusing me?" For a moment his handsome face looked surprised. Then he smiled and slid his sunglasses back on. "You might want to reconsider that."

Kitty narrowed her eyes. "Why?"

"Well . . . about this phony engagement of yours . . ." His voice was pleasant and neutral. "It'd be hard to pull off a successful scam if everybody knows about it, don't you think?" His thin lips curved in a grim smile. "I've always been told I have a tendency to talk too much."

"Three thousand dollars buys your silence, is that it? That's extortion."

Jay shuddered in mock distress. "Extortion. Ugh . . . what an ugly word."

Kitty knew Jay would follow through with his threat. And any gossip about a phony engagement would spread through the small town like wildfire. Jay wouldn't care in the least what became of Lakeview Manor. Everything he cared about began and ended with himself.

Three thousand dollars would send him away happy. But only until the next time he needed money. And there would always be a next time.

Kitty took a deep breath and faced her ex-husband, refusing to cave in to his demands. "You can threaten all you want, Jay. I'm not giving you any money."

Anger flickered across his face. "You think I won't talk?" He took a long, deliberate look at the manor and the lush garden. "It'd be a shame to let this place fall into the hands of that developer."

"You can talk all you want." She stared at him, her gaze cool and steady. "But no one will believe you. I'll deny everything you say. I'll put an announcement of our engagement in the local paper if I have to." She raised her chin stubbornly. For the first time in years she was standing up to Jay Hilliard. "I'll tell the whole world that I'm deeply in love with Keefe Brody, and—"

The breath stopped in her throat. Keefe. Kitty looked at him with wide eyes as he stepped out onto the patio.

"Is there a problem here?" His voice was polite enough, but laced with an edge of steel that Kitty had never heard before.

Jay eyed him warily, but didn't back down. "I'm having a private discussion with my wife, if you don't mind."

"*Ex-wife.*" Keefe stared at Jay, taking all of two seconds to sum him up and form an unflattering opinion. "And I do mind."

Sensing danger, Kitty moved between the two men. "It's all right, Keefe." She laid a hand on his arm. "Jay was just leaving."

A muscle twitched in Jay's jaw and his eyes glittered like ice behind the dark glasses. "We haven't finished our business," he reminded Kitty. "I'm sure you want to give my idea some extra thought."

She shook her head. "My answer is final."

Keefe could feel anger pulse like an electric current through her small hand. He looked down at her flushed face and felt his protective instincts rise. He didn't know the whole story behind her marriage, but he could guess it hadn't been easy. He gave Jay a cold look. "Looks like your business is finished, then."

Jay wasn't about to let three thousand dollars go without a fight. He glared at Kitty, his mouth twisting in an ugly grimace. "You'll wish you gave me that money."

Keefe's eyes narrowed. So this was Jay Hilliard's

business. A shakedown, pure and simple. "What money?"

"This isn't your problem, Keefe." Kitty took a half step toward her ex-husband. "You have to leave now, Jay."

"Maybe it is his problem, after all. Maybe my silence will be worth three thousand dollars to him." He grinned, cocky and self-assured at the prospect of easy money. "What do you say, Brody? Three thousand dollars isn't much."

"Forget it, Jay!" Kitty said warningly.

"No. Let him talk." Keefe's expression went still as he stared at the smaller man. Jay Hilliard was nothing but a two-bit hustler. Since he had taken the trouble to come all the way to Lake George to extort money from his ex-wife, he'd have to go through Keefe to get it. He'd listen to the man. Before he threw him off the property.

"It's very simple," Jay explained, sounding like a consummate businessman about to close an important deal. "I need three thousand dollars. You need the truth about your, uh, engagement kept quiet, if you get what I'm saying."

"Just who do you plan on going to?"

Jay shrugged. "I can start with the local papers. And I'm sure that coffee shop in town is a good place to get some interesting gossip going. What would people say if they heard you were scamming your own mother?" He smiled at Keefe, his face a mask of moral superiority. "Now I don't know about you, but a story about a phony engagement would be sure to catch *my* attention. Might even get picked up by the Associated Press, make the national news . . ."

"The local papers wouldn't print rumors or hearsay," Keefe said. "You have no way to back up your claim. And as far as gossip goes, we'd just deny it. You're only a jealous ex-husband making up stories."

"You're willing to take that chance?"

"Try me." Keefe sure as hell wouldn't knuckle under to any ultimatum. "Now get off my property before I call the police and have you arrested for trespassing."

"You'll regret this." Jay was clenching his fists, glowering at Keefe for a long moment as if he were debating taking a swing at him. Finally, he relaxed his hands and looked at Kitty, his eyes drifting suggestively over her body. "Just how far will you go to play the loving fiancée, baby?" He reached out and brushed his thumb slowly over her lower lip. "I know you'll give him a real good time . . ."

Keefe's hand shot out and grabbed Jay's wrist in a punishing grip, jerking him closer until they stood nose to nose. "Nobody talks to my fiancée that way." His teeth glinted in a frightening smile. "Now get out."

Jay gave a yelp of pain, rubbing his wrist when Keefe released him. He backed away, glaring at them. "You'll pay for that," he vowed, holding his throbbing wrist. "Just wait." Muttering an obscenity, he turned and walked away.

Keefe looked at Kitty. She was staring wide-eyed after Jay, her face pale. He reached out and gently touched her shoulder. "You okay?"

His concern touched a vulnerable spot inside her. She nodded her head. "I'm sorry," she whispered.

"For what? Him?" Keefe shrugged. "It's over now."

Kitty faced him suddenly. "No, it's not. Jay came here for money. And he left humiliated." A breeze blew a lock of hair against her cheek and she shoved at it impatiently. "He won't forget that, Keefe. He'll get even."

"Let me worry about that." He tucked the strand of hair behind her ear. "If he comes back, or contacts you in any way, you let me know."

"Jay is my ex-husband, Keefe." Kitty frowned, looking toward the side of the house as if expecting Jay to appear again. "It's not your problem."

"Well, I've just made him my problem." Keefe took her by the shoulders, swinging her around to face him. "Promise me, Kitty. If he contacts you again, you come to me."

Her blue eyes were troubled, as though she wasn't sure how to let someone else shoulder her burden. Finally, she nodded. "You probably regret the day I came here."

He smiled. "Oh, I don't know. I know you're a good carpenter. And you're cute."

"Cute." Kitty rolled her eyes. "Puppies are cute. Two-year-olds are cute. Thirty-year-old women aren't cute."

He feigned a look of horror. "A hag, to be sure."

She laughed and gave him a playful look, her mood lighter than it had been all day. "You really like making fun of me, don't you?"

"Anything to get a smile out of you."

What he really liked, he thought, was the way sunlight shimmered like liquid gold in her hair. How laughter lit up her face. The way her eyes reminded him of the deep, blue water of the lake. He could tumble in headfirst. . . .

"Let's go for a walk," he suggested.

"I'd like that," she said. She needed a change of scenery, needed to focus on anything but Jay.

With the afternoon sun warm on their shoulders, they walked toward the wooded trail. Keefe reached out and took her hand in a gesture that seemed entirely natural. His hand was strong and large, its warmth distracting her, making her feel scattered and dizzy. She had never felt that way with Jay.

So why was she feeling it now?

She was looking at Keefe in a whole different light, she realized. She'd felt threatened with Jay. And Keefe had been the classic hero, charging to the rescue, taking up the gauntlet like a knight on a white steed. So naturally her emotions were confused right now. Naturally in her vulnerable state she'd find Keefe more . . . *attractive?*

God, she was completely hopeless.

Impatiently, Kitty forced herself to concentrate on the scenery around her. The shady trail meandered through a grove of tall oak and hickory and spruce trees. Ferns and delicate wild geraniums grew along the edge of the path.

The trail led to a sandy clearing by the lake. Gentle waves rolled in rhythmically, lapping the pebbly shore. An aluminum canoe tied to the old wooden dock bobbed up and down on the water.

Keefe stopped at the edge of the clearing. For a long moment he said nothing, drinking in the panorama of deep blue water and pine-covered mountains. The sight never failed to stir a strong sense of pride deep within him.

He turned to look at Kitty, hoping to see the same sense of wonder in her eyes. But she was staring at the ground, yawning as she toed a small stone with her foot.

Her obvious boredom sent a swift bolt of irritation through him, catching him by surprise. He shouldn't care one way or the other how she felt about the land. After all, she was only here for the summer. Yet her reaction left him with a raw ache.

"It won't work," he said, dropping her hand. "If you're bored here, my mother will think we're not suited." Without waiting for her reply, Keefe strode ahead to the dock. Stepping up on the weathered boards, he walked to the end, frowning as he stared out across the water.

They'd been foolish to agree to Beth's little scheme, he realized grimly. Kitty was like every other woman he had dated—unimpressed with what was most important to him. And that one difference alone would make the scam all the harder to pull off.

Kitty followed him onto the dock. "I wasn't bored."

Keefe didn't speak for a long moment. All he could think was that this could well be his last summer here. Wendell Burkett would sign the deed to Lakeview

Manor, and there was nothing he could do to change that.

"Did you hear me?"

"I guess I misread your wild, unbridled enthusiasm," he remarked dryly.

She sighed. "Look, I was tired, okay? I had a long day. Physical work is very tiring. You probably don't understand that, seated behind a desk all day, but—"

He looked at her, laughter in his eyes. "You think I'm a couch potato, is that it?"

"Well, yes, in a way you are. Aside from floating around in a canoe, or whatever it is you do out here, I'm sure your fingers get quite a workout on the keyboard."

He laughed. "Let me assure you, Kitty," he said softly, leaning down to speak close to her ear. "Piloting a canoe can be *very* physical."

His warm breath caressed her cheek and she felt her face heat up in response. She backed up a step. "If you say so," she said a little breathlessly.

Her skepticism made him long to teach her a few things. In a very physical way.

He motioned to the canoe. "Hop in. It's time for your first lesson. Canoeing 101."

"No thanks." She gazed down at the canoe bobbing with each wave, the motion making her slightly seasick. "I'll tip it over, and I . . . I can't swim." She felt embarrassed to admit that. Especially to a man who didn't appear to have any weaknesses of his own.

He motioned to the bottom of the canoe. "If it'll make you feel better, you can put a life jacket on."

She peered down. "There's only one. If we capsize—"

"We won't. Besides, I'm a fairly decent swimmer." He paused a beat. "For a couch potato."

She caught the amusement in his eyes and suddenly had to laugh at herself. Keefe Brody was six feet four of solid, well-toned muscle and probably the most physically fit man she had ever met. "You're not going to let me forget that, are you?"

"Nope." He sat on the edge of the dock and lowered himself into the boat. He stood in the middle, riding the swell of the water as though he'd been born to it. "Come on in. It's as sturdy as an ark."

He wasn't going to give up. Grumbling, Kitty sat down on the planks, dangling her legs over the edge. The waves made gurgling sounds beneath the dock, and she looked at the water as if expecting some sea creature to surface.

Keefe shook his head at her procrastination. Without further ado, he grabbed hold of her upper arm, ignoring her small squeak of protest as he lifted her off the dock. The boat tipped and Kitty lurched forward. She clutched at Keefe's arms to keep from tumbling into the lake. The deep water swelled and splashed, rising perilously close to the rim of the canoe.

"Sturdy as an ark?" She was afraid to move a muscle. "Last time I listen to you."

He laughed as his arms went around her. "So it was a slight exaggeration," he admitted jovially. His hands were resting on the waistband of her jeans. Instinctively, he pulled her a little closer, liking the feel of her in his arms. The faint scent of lavender soap teased his nostrils. A light breeze riffled through her hair, lifting it back from her neck, and he lowered his head, tempted to taste the delicate skin over her collarbone.

Kitty wasn't sure exactly what caused her sudden dizzy spell: the threat of being pitched into the lake or the warmth of Keefe's arms around her. She hoped it wasn't the latter. Pulling away from him, she sat down abruptly on the seat in front.

Keefe grabbed the life jacket and helped Kitty slip her arms through it, then fastened the front ties. "There," he said, smiling gently at the sight of her in the oversize vest. He almost gave in to the urge to kiss her. He cupped her chin in his hand. "Still scared?"

Kitty drew in a deep, unsteady breath. It wasn't the water that scared her. It was Keefe, the touch of his hand on her skin that made her feel vibrantly alive. "I'm all right," she whispered.

"Good." He untied the rope securing the canoe to the dock, then picked up a paddle. "I'll show you how it's done. Pay attention," he teased, taking his seat at the stern. "There might be a test later." With slow, even strokes, he maneuvered them away from the dock.

The canoe skimmed along under Keefe's expert guidance, cutting a silent passage through the water. Kitty couldn't help but exclaim over their surroundings.

"It's so beautiful!" she said, her voice filled with delight. "The sparkling water, the way the mountains come right down to the lake . . . oh, my." She sighed as she looked around in wonder, dazzled by the sunlight, the open spaces and the scenery. Suddenly Jay's reappearance in her life was forgotten. Out here, everything seemed so fresh and new. Like a clean slate. She felt immediately rejuvenated, her spirits lifting as though on the wings of a bird, soaring high up to the clouds.

"Beautiful," she said again.

"You like it?" An unmistakable note of surprise mingled with the pride in Keefe's voice.

"Who on earth wouldn't?"

He shrugged and stopped paddling for a moment, letting the canoe drift with the current. "Some women find nature boring. Or too primal and rugged." He grew quiet. "I love it here. And now I could very well lose it."

"Perhaps your mother was just making idle threats," Kitty said, wanting to say something encouraging, something to give him some small measure of hope. "Maybe she'll realize selling the manor would be a mistake."

Keefe shook his head, a wry smile twisting his mouth. "From a financial standpoint, selling Lakeview Manor would be the smart thing to do. My mother would net a tidy little profit and retire quite comfortably down in Boca."

"But money isn't motivating her to sell, is it?"

"No." Keefe sobered quickly, bitter anger surging like a tide inside him. "The only thing motivating my mother is my bachelor status. I suppose it's her way of teaching me a lesson. Wendell Burkett just happened to show up at the right time. What luck."

Damn. Thinking about it put him in a bad mood. He hated being backed into a corner, and that was precisely what his mother had done to him. Now the fate of his home was staked on some silly game. He bit back the loud curse that hovered on his lips and thrust the wooden oar into the water, using deep, swift strokes to work off his tension.

Kitty held on to her seat as the canoe skimmed forward. "Your mother seems determined to see you married."

"She doesn't approve of my dating habits."

Kitty could see how that might be met with disapproval. But on the other hand, threatening to sell the family home did seem a little extreme. "Maybe if you talk with her, explain how you feel—"

"She's an intelligent woman. She knows how I feel."

"If your mother is so intelligent, don't you think she'll notice that . . . well, that you don't really love me?" Though she had stumbled awkwardly over the words, she held his gaze, waiting for his answer.

"That's why we have to play it right." One dark brow lifted and a rakish smile cut across his face. "Think you can handle it?"

"Sure." Kitty shrugged and faced forward again, dipping her fingers into the cool water, letting them trail idly along the surface. She could put on the appropriate charade when the time came. "I'll do what it takes."

"What it takes, huh?" Keefe's eyes gleamed at the

innocent remark and his imagination went wild. "My mother won't be easy to fool. We'll have to lay it on thick."

"No problem."

"Even if it means spending the night together?"

Her head snapped up at the suggestion and she turned around to glare at him. "It will never mean that."

He laughed, a slow and lazy and infuriatingly seductive sound. "Picture it. You and me, stumbling out of the same bedroom in the morning. Sleepy and rumpled and satisfied. My mother's sure to be convinced."

Kitty's temper flared at the image. "It would convince her I sleep around."

Keefe's eyes glinted. Leaning forward in his seat, he gave her a look of new interest. "Well, do you?"

"Of course not!"

He grinned at her offended expression. "Don't knock what you haven't tried."

"Spoken by someone who *has.*" For the first time she felt sympathy for Mrs. Brody. "That attitude is exactly why you're in this whole predicament."

"I have an attitude?"

"Yes. And because of it, you're in danger of losing what's most important to you. You'd rather pretend you're in a steady relationship than actually work on a real one." She ended her brief lecture with a shake of her head. "You'd better hope your mother doesn't know you're pretending."

"Let me worry about that," he said. "You just concentrate on being sweet and loving. If that's not too much of a stretch for you."

"Oh, I'll be as sweet as honey," she said, ignoring his sarcasm. "But the charade still might not work." She turned and flashed him a smug smile. "Your mother will sell the house anyway when she decides I'm too good for you."

He laughed at that. "That's quite a high horse you've climbed up on, sweetheart."

Sweetheart. The word sounded sour to her ears. "Save the endearment for when we have an audience," she suggested. "Out here it's rather wasted, don't you think?"

"There's nothing wrong with a little practice. We're going to need it in order to pull this show off." He paddled a few more strokes, then added, "It'll take quite a bit of work to convince my mother you're in love with me."

"It would be a whole lot easier to fool your mother if you were a little more agreeable. We'd get along better."

"And you're a real pro at getting along, huh?"

He regretted the words at once. He hadn't been referring to Jay Hilliard and their made-in-hell marriage, but it was plain from the fire smoldering in her eyes that she thought he had. A shaft of guilt seared through him. "Look, Kitty, I'm sorry. I didn't mean—"

"Of course you did." She ignored his apology. "And maybe you're right. Who am I to criticize you? I'm hardly the authority you are on relationships. After all, you've had so much more practice." She faced forward again. "Take me back, please."

Keefe swore under his breath, feeling dismayed by her anger and the apology thrown back in his face. Picking up his paddle, he handed it to her.

She took the paddle from him and turned it over in her hands. "What's this?"

"A wooden implement with a wide, flat blade and long, narrow handle used to pilot a variety of watercraft." He shrugged. "Otherwise known as a paddle."

"Very clever." She was in no mood for levity. "Why are you giving it to me?"

"Best way I know to learn how to canoe."

Seven

"*I* have to paddle us back?" Kitty watched as Keefe settled himself comfortably on his seat. "Fine." She'd get them back. No problem. How hard could it be?

Fixing her eyes on the distant shore, she plunged the paddle into the water and began stroking, trying to copy Keefe's strong, even movements. But her motions were choppy. The canoe didn't glide through the water, as it did with Keefe. It lurched and jerked. She stopped to take a breath, only to realize they had gone nowhere but a complete circle.

Kitty looked around in disbelief. But it was true. All her points of reference were the same. They were floating in the exact spot where she had started.

Unwillingly, she caught Keefe's eye. He was grinning. "Full speed ahead!" he cried, sounding very much like a fleet admiral leading a battalion of warships.

Kitty narrowed her gaze at him and faced forward, jabbing the paddle into the water on the other side of the canoe. This time they turned counterclockwise.

Blinking back tears of frustration, she tried again, paddling first on starboard, then on port side. But she couldn't paddle fast enough. The current was too strong, pulling the canoe in the opposite direction. With every stroke it seemed the shoreline receded into the distance.

She pulled the paddle out of the water, letting out an angry breath. "Don't you dare laugh!"

"I wouldn't think of it."

Silence ruled for a long moment. Kitty could hear the cry of a hawk flying high over their heads, the slap-splash of water against the canoe. And in the distance, the drone of an outboard motor. What she wouldn't give for a motor!

"Well?" she demanded, looking over her shoulder at him. "Aren't you going to say 'I told you so'?"

"I hadn't planned on it."

Kitty faced forward again, still smarting over her unskilled handling of the boat. He probably thought she handled her *tools* in the same inept way. "You were right. I was wrong," she gritted out. "Evidently there is more to steering a canoe than just . . . floating around."

Keefe picked up the extra paddle from the bottom of the canoe. "Then you've just learned your first lesson." He left it at that and began heading home.

By the time they reached the shore, Kitty was in a rotten mood. Before Keefe had finished securing the canoe to the pier, she was scrambling out of the boat onto the dock. She struggled out of the life jacket, tossed it back in the canoe, and stormed up the trail.

Keefe soon caught up. "You know what? If you want to convince my mother we're engaged, you have to stop running away from me in a huff. I gotta tell you—it looks bad."

"Your mother isn't here." Glimpsing the gray stone walls of the manor ahead, she increased her pace.

"What's the hurry?"

She let out her breath in annoyance. "I'm cold, I'd like a shower, and I'm starving." She didn't slow her stride until they reached the house.

Walking inside, Kitty came to a dead halt. The kitchen table had been set for a formal dinner. Two place settings of Helen Brody's good china and silver gleamed in the light. Crystal goblets sparkled next to a bottle of wine.

Keefe spotted a note lying on the counter and picked it up. "Tonight's dinner, compliments of Beth. We're supposed to enjoy the, uh, *pleasure* of each other's company." He shot Kitty a dark look and went to open the refrigerator. "She made us chicken casserole. We just have to reheat it."

"Oh." It was the only response she could manage.

He shut the refrigerator and leaned against it, folding his arms across his chest. "Oh?" he repeated dryly. "Didn't you just say you were starving?"

"It's just that I had other plans." She'd planned on a long hot shower, a quiet evening alone.

"Running away again, Kitty?" His eyes scanned the length of her. "I think you're afraid to pretend you're going to marry me. You're afraid to get to know me better."

"You forget I learned quite a bit last night."

"And what have I learned about you? Not enough

to warrant a serious marriage proposal. And my mother will notice that immediately."

He was right. Kitty hated to admit it. "All right," she sighed. "But I'm showering first."

And as she headed upstairs to her room, Kitty realized that Beth had succeeded again. With nothing more than a simple note and a homecooked meal, she'd gotten them to spend another evening together.

Dinner was served, wine poured and a salad tossed by the time Kitty returned. While she'd been showering Keefe had changed into khaki slacks and a shortsleeve shirt with a wild jungle print. The shirt was half unbuttoned, showing a distracting portion of muscled chest.

Kitty jerked her gaze away. She'd seen plenty of male chests before. So she could just keep her eyes to herself. Besides, it wasn't like she was attracted to him. No way.

"Hungry?" he asked, glancing over to where she stood in the doorway. She wore a pale apricot pullover with matching leggings. The light cotton fabric clung to her body, making her look soft and feminine, as fresh as a spring flower. She smelled like spring flowers, too. He caught the faint scent of honeysuckle as she walked past him to the table.

"Starved," she admitted as she took her seat.

Keefe tossed the hot pads on the counter and sat down.

"Tonight is Ladies Night," he declared, dishing up

a healthy portion onto her plate. "We talk only about Kitty."

"It'll be a short conversation." She raised a warning hand and grinned at him. "No jokes about my size, please."

He laughed as he helped himself to the salad. "I have nothing but compliments about your size."

His gaze drifted over her in approval, and Kitty felt her cheeks heat up in response. She was relieved when he didn't go into more detail.

"Tell me about yourself," he said simply.

Slowly, with Keefe's gentle coaching, Kitty told him of her life in Philadelphia, the hustle and bustle of the city streets, a fast-paced world so different from Lake George.

"Do you prefer the city?" he asked.

She shook her head. "It's convenient for working. I have to live where the jobs are. And there are a lot of people—especially in the Old City section—who want historic renovations done." She described some of the more vintage buildings, the town houses that dated from before the American Revolution. "I get a lot of input from the Historical Society. I always research the structure first. Wherever possible, I restore rather than tear down." An animated look came over her face as she talked. "Some of the homes are so historically accurate, it's like stepping back in time! You'd almost expect to bump into Thomas Jefferson."

A smile tipped the corner of his mouth. He found her enthusiasm charming. And contagious. He thought he was the only one who found history fascinating. "You ought to come to my class and give a talk on historic architecture."

"Or you could bring them to the city on a field trip," she suggested. "Take them to Independence Hall. The Betsy Ross House. They'd get a real hands-on lesson."

"Thirty rowdy freshmen on the loose in Philadelphia . . ." He pretended to shudder. "I'm not paid enough."

"Have you ever been to Philadelphia?"

Keefe nodded. "I had a two-day conference at the University of Pennsylvania. Beth took a day off from work and dragged me all over town, sightseeing." He paused to pour more wine into their glasses. "Last November."

November. She vaguely remembered Beth mentioning an out-of-town visitor. But she'd been dealing with her divorce then. Keefe had been in her neighborhood, walking the streets of her town. And she'd been totally unaware of it. For some strange reason, Kitty felt cheated.

"How did you meet Beth?" Keefe asked a moment later.

"College. We were assigned the same dorm room." She jabbed a piece of chicken with her fork, thinking back to her college days. "Beth was like nobody I had ever met. There was never a dull moment on campus! She had a flair for the dramatic. I told her she should have majored in Theater Arts."

"Believe it or not, college toned her down." Keefe helped himself to another serving of chicken, between bites telling Kitty about his childhood at

Lakeview Manor, especially some of the more amusing escapades with Beth.

"I'll never forget the look on my mother's face when she opened the refrigerator and saw the bucket of bait Beth had put inside, right next to the fancy canapés Mother had planned to serve at her Garden Club tea. Mother was always hosting luncheons or local charity fund-raisers here." He chuckled at the memory. "Beth was determined to keep her bait fresh for our next fishing trip. She thought she'd slip the bucket out before anyone noticed it. The smell of worms and dead minnows permeated everything."

Kitty wrinkled her nose and felt a rush of sympathy for Mrs. Brody. "Beth always jumps into things without thinking about the consequences," she remarked. "One time at college she brought one of those dribble glasses to a frat party as a practical joke. Somehow the glass got misplaced and ended up in the faculty lounge."

"Don't tell me. One of the teachers used it."

Kitty grinned. "The dean himself. It was horrible— orange juice all down his shirt. Beth got blamed for it."

Keefe finished his dinner and pushed his plate back. "I'll bet you never expected she'd involve you in anything other than the renovation job when you came here."

"With Beth I've learned to expect the unexpected." Kitty rose from the table, carrying her empty plate to the sink. "But she's a good-hearted person. She helped me tough out a bad situation."

"Meaning your ex-husband."

"Don't tell Beth he was here." She collected the rest of the dishes and looked at Keefe, her eyes softly pleading. "If she finds out Jay came all the way to Lake George, she'd stop seeing Tom just to stay home and worry over me."

One look into her wide, blue eyes and Keefe knew he'd agree to anything. "If that's the way you want it."

He rose from the table and moved to the counter, watching her work at the sink. He wondered how in the world an intelligent, beautiful woman like Kitty O'Neill had ever ended up with such a despicable character. Curiosity burned through him until he couldn't hold back the question any longer. "Why did you marry that man, Kitty?"

"Not one of my smartest decisions, was it?" A half smile flirted at the edges of her mouth. She closed her eyes briefly. "I thought I was in love with him. I thought he loved me. We married too soon, before I really . . . knew him. Talk about a whirlwind courtship! I guess I got swept away by the romance of it all." She sighed. "Jay was handsome and exciting. And so charming! He knew all the right things to say. I felt like the most cherished woman on earth."

"The man you marry should make you feel that way."

"But with Jay it was all a line." She stared out the darkened window over the sink, seeing nothing but the past. It still amazed her to know that there hadn't been one honest thing about their relationship.

"What happened?"

Kitty shrugged. "We grew apart," she said, her lips curving as she searched for humor in a situation that had been anything but funny. "We had different goals. I wanted to earn money to start my own business. Jay wanted to run up my charge cards and drain my bank account."

Keefe eased a low whistle through his teeth. The past few years had been hard for her. He had to stop himself from reaching out, putting his arms around her. "Sounds like you were taken for a ride," he said gently.

"I was so stupid!" she whispered impatiently.

"Not stupid. Just . . . blind. Love does that to a person." He had a strong urge to go find Jay Hilliard and pummel him.

"Beth warned me. I should have listened to her."

"I take it she didn't like him."

Kitty laughed at the understatement. "She thought he was too smooth, like he was hiding something. He said he was an investor, and I believed him. He'd turn up with wads of cash, and I just figured . . ." She sighed at her ignorance.

"He wasn't investing in mutual funds, I gather."

Kitty smiled. "No. More like horses and numbers." She paused, thoughtful. "I didn't find that out until after we were married. I also didn't know he'd been married twice before. He owed both his ex-wives a lot of money, but they had no legal grounds to make him pay."

She grabbed the dish detergent, giving Keefe a wry smile. "And here he was today. Up to his old tricks."

Keefe recorked the wine and put it in the refrigerator. "He won't come back. Not if he knows what's good for him."

Kitty turned away and filled the sink with soapy water. "I hope you're right." She began scrubbing the plates.

Keefe grabbed a dishtowel and began drying the dishes, smiling as he realized with no small amount of irony how much they resembled an old married couple, doing basic, everyday chores together.

That very thought struck Kitty at the same time. She grinned over at him and handed him a wet plate. "We'll have to be sure to do this when your mother's here. Staying home on a Saturday night, doing the dishes. I think she'll be quite convinced we're headed toward marital bliss."

"There are other ways to convince my mother we're in love." Keefe finished drying the plate and set it aside.

"Like how?" Kitty asked absently, all her attention focused on scrubbing the casserole dish. "Holding hands?"

"No." Keefe took the wet dish from her hands and slowly wiped it dry. He glanced sideways at Kitty, his gaze drawn to her mouth. She seemed lost in thought, her lower lip caught between her teeth while she wrung out the dishcloth. "I was thinking more along the lines of kissing," he said. "We should try one now. For practice."

Kitty's fingers lost their grip on the cloth. It fell with a plop into the soapy water. "I . . . don't see why that would be necessary."

"We should rehearse our technique, make it look legitimate. Kissing can be a complicated thing, you know." He was smiling as he looked down into her stunned face. His suggestion had shocked her. "We wouldn't want to bump noses or look like we don't know what we're doing, would we?"

"I think we can manage to . . . to act like we're engaged without actually kissing," she stammered. Really, Kitty thought, he was carrying the scam a little too far.

"If we really were engaged you would have been kissed by now. Kissed often and kissed thoroughly. Kissed in the morning, kissed at night—"

She felt her cheeks begin to blaze. "Stop saying that word!" Her eyes dropped to his mouth. Quickly, she jerked her gaze away and faced the sink again.

"What word?"

"Kiss!" Flustered, she began moving her hands. "Or kissing, or kissed . . ." Her whole body seemed to be on fire.

"Why, Miss O'Neill," he said, looking pleasantly surprised. "The thought of kissing me makes you nervous."

Kitty tried to scoff at that. "Why should it?"

He folded his arms and studied her profile, the small, pretty nose, the full mouth that looked very kissable. "Because you might like it."

"You are so conceited!" Kitty retrieved the cloth, wrung it out and began wiping off already spotless counters. She needed something to do with her hands.

"Most women I know enjoy kissing."

"One kiss is just like any other," she stated primly, trying not to think of the quick, passionless pecks Jay had given her whenever he had wanted something.

"Had one kiss, you've had them all. They're the same."

Casually Keefe plucked the cloth from her grip and laid it on the counter. "How about it? One simple kiss. If it's the same as any other, we won't kiss anymore."

The man wasn't going to give up. "Oh, all right! But only one," she warned him.

He planted his hands on the edge of the counter, one on either side of her. "Ready?"

She moistened her lower lip, feeling unbearably nervous. "Yes," she whispered. "If you really want to . . ."

If he really wanted to! He'd always wanted to kiss her. He leaned in the rest of the way and lightly touched his mouth to hers.

Kitty gave a small gasp of surprise and quickly broke contact. She had fully expected to feel nothing. Instead, the gentle touch of his lips against hers seemed to affect her whole body. She leaned hard against the counter and stared at him, shaken.

"Was it that bad?" Keefe eased back a bit, looking down at her with amusement. "You hardly gave me time to—"

"It was . . . the same . . ." But the tremor in her voice said otherwise.

He shook his head. "Then I'll just have to change your mind." Before she could stop him, he slid his hands behind her waist, dragging her away from the counter and straight into his arms. As his mouth took possession of hers, every ounce of her willpower evaporated in the heat of desire. Kitty melted in his arms and kissed him back.

And knew nothing between them would ever be the same.

She moaned softly against his mouth, unable to stop herself from responding. She slid her hands, palms flat, over the fabric of his shirt, reveling in the feel of him, tracing the solid muscles of his chest. When she reached the opening of his shirt, her hands stilled for a brief instant. But she needed to touch him, to feel the heat of his flesh. Her fingers slipped beneath the fabric, skimming over warm male skin. She heard his sharp intake of breath.

He broke off the kiss and his gaze locked on hers. His eyes were hot, glittering with passion, the unspoken message in them enflaming her.

"I like the feel of you in my arms," he murmured in a voice that intoxicated her like wine. "I like it when you touch me . . ." His mouth lowered to kiss the soft flesh of her throat, then moved lazily to suck gently at her earlobe.

Kitty's head tilted back, need and desire overruling common sense. She thought her bones had turned to liquid as his hands slid down her back and over her hips, working their erotic magic. She offered no resistance when he lifted the hem of her pullover. She was beyond thought, eager for his touch, waiting for it with breathless anticipation.

When it came, a feather-light touch against her breast, she gasped softly and arched into him. Encouraged, he cupped one breast, filling his palm with the weight of it. Then his fingers dipped down, deftly unhooking the front clasp of her bra, peeling the lacy cup aside. His thumb brushed over her exposed nipple, teasing the small bud to life. Cool air tingled her sensitive flesh.

She shivered and lifted her eyes to his. For one long, tense moment they stared at each other. She felt confused and dizzy, as if she had just awakened from a dream.

What are we doing?

How had one little practice kiss led to such a wild yearning for more?

She shook her head, stunned to realize how much she had wanted him. And beyond all reason, too. They didn't even get along, for one thing. Couldn't spend much time together without arguing. And here she was, losing all sense of control at the first touch of his lips.

"Kitty . . ." The deep, rough timbre of his voice washed over her, making her tremble as she watched his mouth form her name. His beautiful, masculine, sensuous mouth. And she very nearly kissed him again.

Oh, no, she thought in agony. This was insane. She made a small sound of dismay and closed her eyes, swaying against him. She felt his arms tighten around her, his thigh move against hers. Her whole body was so sensitive to his touch that the slightest caress of his fingertips was enough to make every nerve ending hum.

She shouldn't let him continue, shouldn't want . . . *this.* Especially with a man who'd never be anything more than an accomplice in Beth's absurd hoax.

"We shouldn't . . . do this," she whispered bro-kenly.

He gave a shaky laugh. "Apparently we don't need any practice, after all." His voice was low and dark and as seductive as midnight. He began pulling her closer again.

She edged away, stepping out of the circle of his arms, reminding herself that there was nothing be-tween them but a charade. And that was all there'd ever be.

"Then we should stop. As you said, we don't need practice." She folded her arms and looked up at him, coming to a decision. They'd have to find some other way to convince Mrs. Brody they were in love. "I've decided we won't be doing any more kissing."

"*You've* decided?" He seemed amused at that.

"It's better this way, Keefe. Less chance of us get-ting, you know . . . *involved.* More than we need to be." She caught herself gesturing with her hands and clasped them in front of her. "I mean, look at us. Our whole relationship is phony. Plus we got off to such a bad start. You didn't want me here—"

"Have I asked you to leave?" he inquired in a silky voice.

"Well, no," she admitted. "But we don't really like each other. We always argue."

"I prefer to think of it as healthy discussion. It doesn't mean we can't like each other."

"But if it weren't for the threat of losing Lakeview Manor, we'd have nothing to do with each other. We'd be busy doing other things." She didn't wait for him to confirm or deny that. She knew she was right. "Do you understand what I'm saying?"

"I'm not to kiss you."

"Exactly." It *was* better that way, Kitty told herself. She couldn't risk another kiss like the one Keefe had given her. The effects had been . . . dangerous. Even Jay Hilliard on their wedding day hadn't made her feel like that. With Keefe it had been too real—and much too passionate for two people who weren't even close to being in love. Besides, she knew how easily one kiss could lead to other things. "So. You agree, then."

His gaze raked over her face. The desire to kiss her again still raged through him. But she wanted none of it. In fact, the prospect of *not* kissing made her look just a little too relieved. A muscle ticked in his jaw and his eyes went hard. "And blow the whole game? No."

She stared at him, surprised. "No?"

"That's right." He had no intention of maintaining a platonic relationship. That would send up red flags like nothing else. "My mother's suspicions would be aroused if this engagement didn't have a normal amount of intimacy."

"Beth said nothing about—"

"This doesn't involve Beth anymore," Keefe cut in. "The game is between you and me now." He studied her for a long moment. "Are you still in on it?"

Kitty thought of her promise to Beth. She was basically trapped, no doubt about it. "I . . . yes."

"Then if I have to kiss you, I will."

Kitty hated feeling powerless. He was calling the

shots now, and there was nothing she could do about it. "I suppose next you'll want us to pretend we spend the night in the same bedroom."

"When we spend the night together, Kitty, you'll know why I'm there. And I won't be pretending."

That shocked the breath out of her. He'd said *when*. Not *if*. She turned and walked to the hallway, trying not to tremble. "It's late. I'm going to bed."

"What, no goodnight kiss?"

She paused to give him a withering look. "Save it for when it counts."

"Don't act like you didn't like it, Kitty."

"But I didn't like it, Keefe." She spoke the lie evenly. "It was exactly like any other kiss, as I expected. I was just pretending. If I've fooled *you*, then we don't have a thing to worry about when your mother's here."

Without another word she turned and walked away.

Eight

"Keefe went to Albany three days ago and hasn't come back!" Beth fretted. "What did you do to make him leave?"

Kitty stopped hammering, shrugging a shoulder as she faced her friend. "Nothing." She gripped the hammer a little tighter as a wave of guilt hit her full force. She hadn't seen Keefe since Saturday night when he had kissed her. When she had lied and told him she didn't like it.

"I don't believe it." Beth folded her arms and began pacing, the slap of her leather sandals echoing in the solarium. "He must be avoiding you. Something must have happened while I wasn't here. I can't get ahold of him. There's no answer at his town house and he hasn't been in his office. Oh, I knew I shouldn't have gone out with Tom!"

"Beth, you're overreacting—"

"Am I?" She shot Kitty an accusing glare. "Every time I leave you two alone, you end up at each other's throats. Now Keefe's gone, and Aunt Helen is due to arrive!"

"*What?*" Kitty said in surprise. "But you said she wouldn't come till July!"

"She called this morning. She's coming on Saturday."

"But that's only four days away!" It was too soon. They weren't ready. She felt suddenly like an actress standing on stage with the curtain rising and no lines memorized.

"How's it going to look when she arrives?" Beth fumed. "You and Keefe are supposed to be engaged, and you can't even manage to stay together in the same house!"

"It's not my fault he ran off." Kitty squared her shoulders defensively. "His guilty conscience probably got the better of him. He was acting . . . inappropriately."

"What did he do?"

Kitty sniffed and went back to work. "He kissed me."

Beth stared at Kitty for a full ten seconds. "That's it? That's all?" Her voice rang with sarcasm above the pounding of Kitty's hammer. "The man ought to be arrested!"

Kitty shot her a look. "He kissed me like he—like he meant it." She set another nail and tried to pound it into the window trim. But a strange weakness came over her and her arm refused to cooperate.

Trying not to think of the kiss, she gritted her teeth, using all her strength to drive the nail home. Imagine if Mrs. Brody had seen that little display, Kitty thought in perverse amusement. A wedding announcement would have been placed in the local church paper in no time.

"So what if he did mean it?" Beth asked at last. "What's so bad about one kiss?"

"It was more than one, Beth. And he thinks we should kiss more often. For effect."

"Hmmm . . ." Beth narrowed her eyes, liking the idea. "He's right. It would make things more realistic."

Realistic or not, it didn't make Kitty feel any more comfortable. "Well, I'm not doing it."

Beth frowned in disapproval. "You promised to help. I can't believe you'd jeopardize Lakeview Manor just because you don't want to kiss him!"

Kitty flinched. Now she felt guilty about the way she had acted. If she wasn't careful, Helen Brody would see clear through their little scheme.

But she didn't want to think about any of that now. She didn't want to think about Keefe Brody or the feel of his strong arms around her. Or the desire that had stirred inside when he had kissed her.

She had to concentrate only on why she had been hired without any other issues slowing her down.

Dodging her friend's sharp gaze, Kitty lined up the nail and drove it into the trim with three solid blows, effectively ending their discussion. She smoothed her hand over the pale wood, then stepped back from the window to check her work. Good, she thought in satisfaction. Nice and straight. Just to make sure, she reached for her two-foot level and held it alongside the trim. Perfect.

Beth sighed wearily. "I'm going to try calling him again." Her voice was heavy with hopelessness. "You two need to be together or my plan won't work!"

The next few days had Kitty up to her elbows in renovation work. And although she told herself over and over that it was good to get some serious work done without Beth's plan getting in the way, she still found herself thinking about Keefe, glancing up at the doorway, hoping he'd be there. And she stopped working four times. Actually shut off her circular saw and walked out into the hallway. Simply because she thought she had heard his voice.

By Friday Kitty was utterly miserable.

Keefe parked the Jeep in front of his town house and shut off the motor. He sat back in his seat, forcing himself to breathe slowly. The drive from the university had only added to his tension. Traffic had been heavier than usual, the start of the Memorial Day weekend prompting everyone to knock off work by noon. Cars, trucks, and recreational vehicles had been out in record force, cruising the streets of Albany at a snail's pace, snarling the intersections.

He tried not to think of the quiet solitude at Lakeview Manor. Or the reason he had spent the week away from it. But he had only to close his eyes and he'd see Kitty, all slim curves and tousled blond hair. And soft, kissable mouth.

He couldn't get her off his mind. Not since the night he had held her in his arms and kissed her.

Damn, he thought, remembering that night with a fresh wave of desire. What had he been thinking, kissing her like that? Holding her so closely he had felt every soft, feminine curve. He was tempting himself with something he could never have.

After all, he reminded himself ruthlessly, the kiss had meant nothing to her. Just part of the illusion. He was the one who'd wanted it to lead to something more.

He rubbed a hand over his face, feeling the beginnings of a major headache. None of this was supposed to happen. Any attraction he had for Kitty was supposed to be a complete fabrication. A convincing performance for his mother's benefit. It was obvious where any real attraction would lead.

Exactly nowhere.

Because by the end of the summer, Kitty would be back in Philadelphia and he'd be getting ready to teach a whole new freshman class. His mother, if things went according to plan, would be happily settled in Boca Raton, satisfied with her son's long engagement. And Wendell Burkett would be busy looking for another piece of real estate to exploit.

All those loose ends tied up nice and neat.

Wasn't that what he wanted?

Keefe exhaled heavily and shook his head. He didn't know what he wanted any more. He gathered up his books and research papers from the front seat. He was behind in his work, even after a week of burning the midnight oil at the university. And was it any wonder? His mind hadn't been on his work. Look what he was doing now. Sitting in his Jeep thinking about a certain blond, blue-eyed woman.

This was a definite regression to adolescence, he

thought, making a sound of disgust as he headed inside.

He dropped his books on the couch and fixed himself a quick sandwich. He was just about to sort through his mail when the phone rang. He grabbed the receiver.

"I've been calling you all week!" It was Beth, sounding extremely irritated. "You've got to come back! In case you've forgotten, you're supposed to be engaged."

"I haven't forgotten." He laughed and shifted the phone to his other ear. "We have a long-distance relationship. We get along better with a few miles between us."

"This is no time for jokes," Beth said coolly. "Your mother has had a change of plans. She's not waiting until July. She's coming home tomorrow."

Keefe swore softly. Trust his mother to complicate matters! He and Kitty definitely needed more time to work the kinks out of their relationship.

"Listen, I have to leave," Beth was saying into the phone. "I'm meeting Tom for lunch. When can you get here?"

"I'm on my way."

Kitty brushed sawdust off her jeans and pulled the plug on her sander. She had made more progress in the solarium than she had expected. The three doorways and all the windows had been framed with custom woodwork—exact replicas of the elaborate trim that had graced the manor at the turn of the century.

Nail holes had been patched, rough edges sanded, the surface of the wood ready for the first coat of primer. Next week she would cut and fit the new wainscoting.

She walked around the perimeter of the room, eyeing the pale trim, checking each mitered joint. She ran a hand over a new windowsill, skimming her fingers lightly against the sun-warmed pine.

She sighed, feeling on edge. The basic simplicity of working with her hands usually had a therapeutic effect on her. A job done well always buoyed her spirits, gave her a sense of pride and accomplishment. Her work had been her lifeline while her marriage had crumbled.

So why wasn't she feeling some of that magic now?

It was too quiet at the manor. It gave her too much opportunity to dwell on troubling thoughts. Such as Helen Brody's arrival tomorrow, and Keefe being gone all week. And the reason he had left.

Beth was right, Kitty had to admit. It was her fault. She had driven him away; she had lied to him, insulted him. She could hardly blame him for wanting to leave.

With a sigh she began picking up her tools and placing them in the organized compartments of her toolbox. Why couldn't she stop thinking about Keefe? It was crazy. She hadn't seen him all week. She should have been glad to have had the whole week to work without distraction.

Still, there was this lingering sense of awareness she couldn't shake. It was as if one kiss had put her under some strange spell.

Feeling the need to revive herself, she ducked into

the small powder room just down the hall from the solarium. After splashing water on her face and running her fingers through her hair, she stepped outside to clear her head.

It was a lovely afternoon, the air soft and warm and fragrant with flowers, the blue sky streaked with feathery clouds. Kitty wandered across the lawn toward the woods, her work boots making small indentations in the springy grass. Leaves fluttered in the breeze, revealing shiny patches of the lake. Before she knew it she was following the same path she had taken the week before with Keefe.

She spied the dock up ahead when she reached the clearing. Keefe had pulled his canoe out of the water and turned it upside down. The boat looked forlorn lying there. Unused, abandoned. Kitty couldn't bear to look at it.

What did you do to make him leave . . . ?

Guilt swelled inside her. She had overreacted to a simple kiss. What was the big deal about kissing Keefe Brody? It was just a kiss. So what? People kissed every day.

But to be completely honest with herself, it wasn't the kiss that had her concerned as much as her response to it.

She hadn't wanted it to stop.

Feeling unsettled and oddly lonely, she stepped up onto the dock and walked to the end, the weathered boards creaking under her feet. There were more boats than usual out on the lake, Memorial Day weekend heralding the start of the busy tourist season, but they remained far in the distance. Kitty could make out more than a dozen boats drifting back and forth, their sails like small white triangles against the blue water.

She counted them. Fifteen . . . sixteen . . . seventeen sailboats in all. And then she counted them again, just to give her mind something to focus on. It really was a perfect afternoon to be out on the lake, she thought. If Keefe were here, he'd surely—

No. Counting sailboats wasn't working. Thoughts of Keefe had been surfacing all week, day and night, bringing an uncomfortable mix of emotions that churned inside her. She struggled to concentrate on the scenery, the here and now. The warmth of the sun on her head. The rhythmic slap of water against the dock.

A light breeze caressed her skin, and she turned her face into it, letting it lift the ends of her hair. She stared past the water where massive green mountains brushed the clouds. The view was solid and reassuring and she could feel herself slowly absorb some of that serenity.

She sighed and turned to go, taking only one step before she stopped abruptly, her pulse giving an erratic leap. Keefe stood at the end of the dock, watching her. She stared back at him, forgetting to breathe, the sight of him making her heart pound so fast she felt dizzy. The time spent apart hadn't lessened the impact of his presence. He still had the power, like no other man, to make her weak in the knees.

Of course she could be suffering from some form of sunstroke, she reasoned, trying to explain away this disturbing phenomenon.

Slowly he stepped up onto the dock and came toward her, his gaze holding hers. *God*, he thought, *she is beautiful*. He had spent the last week thinking about her, hoping time apart would cool this attraction he felt for her, get her out of his system. But nothing had changed. He knew that just by looking at her. He still wanted her.

He reached out, almost touching her shoulder, then thought better of it. He already knew how she'd react if he came on too strong. The last thing he wanted was to push Kitty away. He shoved both hands into the pockets of his jeans and smiled down at her.

"I thought I'd find you here."

"I was counting sailboats." She laughed quietly, wondering why she didn't feel the least bit silly. Somehow she knew he'd understand. "Beth reached you, I guess."

He nodded. "She's back at the house now. She's ordered Chinese takeout for dinner. For all of us. Are you hungry?"

"Starved." Her smile faded a bit. "Your mother arrives tomorrow."

"Looks like the show goes on a little sooner than we anticipated."

"Tomorrow is sooner than July, yes." She grew pensive as she realized all over again just how ill-prepared she was for her role as Keefe's fiancée.

"Are you ready?"

Kitty wasn't sure she could handle it. The scam no longer seemed as simple as Beth had assured her it would be. Everything had changed the moment Keefe had kissed her. Now she was feeling things she hadn't felt before. Things she hadn't even felt with the man she had married. It was exhilarating and frightening at the same time.

But those feelings had to be kept under control. She simply wouldn't allow herself to be affected by Keefe—no matter how realistic their little deception might seem.

"I think so." She took a deep breath and lifted her chin. "But we'll need to set some guidelines, some rules of conduct if we're to proceed."

"Such as?"

"For one, I think we should avoid any mention of my ex-husband. If your mother knew of my recent divorce, she'd wonder why I'm so quick to remarry."

"Fair enough," he agreed. Talking about her ex-husband left a bitter taste in his mouth anyway. "What else?"

"You're not to voice your doubts about my professional qualifications to your mother, or question her sanity in hiring me to renovate the west wing."

Keefe's eyes were twinkling. "Would I do that?"

"Every chance you get! If we were truly engaged, you'd approve of my work one hundred and ten percent. So no more potshots at my career."

He fought back a smile. "You will be treated with the respect befitting the future Mrs. Keefe Brody."

She nodded, satisfied. "You learn fast, professor."

"Anything else?"

"Well . . . there is one other thing . . ." She willed herself not to blush. She had to be straightforward about this if they were to continue to play their roles. "About the level of intimacy in our relationship—"

"You mean the kissing."

"Yes."

"We've been through this. You don't want to."

"Actually, I've spent the week thinking about it, and—" She broke off and lowered her eyes, keeping them focused on the rough planks of the dock. For the life of her, she couldn't hold his gaze.

Keefe watched as a delicate blush bloomed over her cheeks and his pulse picked up an extra beat. "Go on."

"Well, Beth sort of convinced me that our engagement would be much more realistic if we . . . kissed now and then."

"That Beth." He owed her big on this one.

"So . . . for the sake of the manor . . ." She reached up to tuck a strand of hair behind her ear, her hand gesturing nervously as she continued to explain. "Maybe a quick, friendly kiss now and then wouldn't hurt. When your mother's around. If the situation calls for it, that is."

She met his eyes then, looking embarrassed and unsure and so damn pretty his mind was spinning.

Very gently he reached out, pulling her into his arms as his mouth lowered to capture hers. The kiss was slow and tender, as if they had all the time in the world. Kitty trembled as her breasts brushed his chest, her earlier resolve to remain unaffected entirely forgotten.

She was breathless when he finally released her. "What was that for?" she managed. There was no one around to see them. No one to impress.

His eyes turned a very dark green. "The situation

called for it," he growled. He took her hand and placed it in the crook of his arm, a courtly gesture that would have won the approval of Helen Brody. "Now, let's go eat."

On Saturday a gentle rain fell shortly before dawn, drenching the lawn and flowers. By the time the sun had peeked over rose-tinged clouds the yard and garden seemed energized with an extra burst of color— the vivid green of the grass, the deep purple of the pansies, the blood red of the geraniums.

Kitty had spent the morning with Beth tidying up the solarium, sweeping out all traces of sawdust, overseeing the removal of the stacks of old paneling— courtesy of the local trash hauler. While her work was nowhere near completion, she and Beth had succeeded in giving the large, airy room a sense of ordered accomplishment. Kitty felt confident that Mrs. Brody would be pleased with the renovation in progress.

After a quick lunch, Kitty showered and put on a fresh outfit, preparing herself both physically and mentally for her first meeting with Mrs. Brody, who was due to arrive sometime in the early afternoon. Dressed in neatly pressed khaki pants and a white blouse, her hair brushed back to fall in a loose wave at her shoulders, she looked cool and unruffled, although the impression was at complete variance with the nerves that were jumping inside her.

She had just met Beth in the hallway outside her

room when a taxicab, brakes squealing, pulled to a stop on the curve of the driveway.

Beth raced over to an alcove window to peer down on the driveway. Quickly, she motioned Kitty over. "She's here!"

Kitty edged closer, watching as a fashionably dressed older woman paid the cabdriver, then headed up the steps to the front door. The driver unloaded four burgundy leather suitcases and trailed Mrs. Brody inside. A moment later he came back out again.

Panic swelled inside Kitty as the cab pulled away. Now that the time had come to put their plan into action, it all seemed like a terrible mistake.

She swallowed and looked at Beth for reassurance. "What if she doesn't like me?"

"Trust me. She'll be thrilled with the idea of you for a daughter-in-law."

"But what if she figures out it's all a scam?" She had a sudden, horrifying image of a furious Helen Brody kicking her out of Lakeview Manor and tossing all her tools after her.

Beth gripped Kitty by the arms. "Calm down. You're just having opening night jitters. Everything will be fine!"

But Kitty remained unconvinced. She stared at Beth with wide eyes, her stomach doing some impressive flips. "I can't believe I let you talk me into doing this," she whispered. "What's next? Robbing banks?" She was feeling slightly hysterical.

"Pull yourself together!" Beth hissed, giving her a quick shake. "You can't back out now!" She pressed her lips together and inhaled deeply through her nostrils. "Okay. We've got to go downstairs. Remember, you're in love with Keefe. You're going to marry him. And you're happy to see his mother, who you've been dying to meet."

Kitty shivered. "Dying is an appropriate word."

"Oh, God." Beth groaned at the sight of Kitty's pale complexion. "You'd better let me do the talking."

They started down the stairs, Beth in front, Kitty feeling as if she were being led to the gallows. As she descended the last step leading into the foyer, the sound of voices caught her ear. Keefe had come into the foyer.

Walking over to Kitty, he slipped an arm around her waist and brushed his lips against her temple, a display that had Beth grinning from ear to ear.

"Darling, I'd like you to meet my mother."

Nine

Helen Brody was tall and elegant and looked at least a decade younger than her sixty-two years. Her glossy silver hair was short and artfully coiffed to sweep away from her face. She wore a pale blue suit tailored in the latest style. The peach and blue scarf tied loosely at her throat framed a flawless complexion unmarred by the Florida sun. She radiated confidence and dignity and a keen intelligence.

She would not be fooled easily. Kitty knew it instinctively. Ignoring the prickle of uneasiness that moved up her spine, she concentrated on maintaining her own poise.

Keefe gave her an encouraging squeeze. "Mother, my fiancée, Kitty O'Neill."

"It's a pleasure to meet you, Mrs. Brody," Kitty murmured, trying to tamp down her rising anxiety. She hoped she didn't sound as nervous as she felt.

Helen took Kitty's hand in a gentle grip and smiled at her. "So this is the young woman who has finally gotten Keefe to forsake bachelorhood." Her green eyes twinkled merrily. "I'd almost given up hope seeing him married."

Beth grinned. "He's been waiting for the right woman."

"Then it was lucky Keefe was in Philadelphia last November," Helen remarked to Kitty. "I'm so glad Beth was able to introduce you two."

Kitty smiled weakly at the bald-faced lie, trying to ignore the twinge to her conscience. Now was not the time to be swayed by guilt. She had a role to play. "Beth was determined that Keefe and I . . . get to know each other," she replied, knowing that explanation, at least, was truthful.

"Well, I just *knew* they were meant to be together," Beth added shamelessly. "It was love at first sight, too. You could even say Kitty was swept off her feet!"

Kitty's cheeks went pink. To her relief, Keefe changed the subject. "Let me help with your luggage, Mother."

"The bags are heavy," Helen cautioned. "I've packed enough for the summer."

Keefe's brow lifted in question. "The summer?"

"I was thinking this morning that three days at Lakeview Manor won't be enough." Helen beamed at the three of them. "I'll be staying till September. It'll give me plenty of time to visit with all of you and get to know my future daughter-in-law. What fun we'll have!"

For a moment everyone was speechless. Kitty saw Keefe's eyes widen slightly, but he recovered quickly. "An excellent idea, Mother," he said smoothly. "We're all looking forward to a nice, long visit."

"Thank you, dear," Helen replied. "Now, if you

FOOL FOR LOVE   141

don't mind, I should start unpacking. I'd like to freshen up."

As soon as Keefe and his mother left the foyer, Kitty rounded on her friend, her blue eyes turbulent. "September?" she whispered querulously. She might have been able to play their charade for a day or two, as Beth had promised, but the whole summer? Anything could go wrong in that amount of time. "Your aunt is bound to realize this is all a big lie."

"I can tell she approves of you already," Beth said cheerily. "What if she does stay for the summer? You and Keefe will just have to be nice to each other a little longer. Aunt Helen will be sure to think you two are the most perfect couple since Adam and Eve."

"Adam and Eve were banished from their home, Beth!"

"Oh, don't be so literal!" She grabbed Kitty's arm and propelled her toward the kitchen. "Come on . . . let's figure out what to make for dinner. I want it to be something special. After all, we're celebrating your engagement!"

"She's quite lovely, Keefe," Helen Brody remarked to her son as they strolled slowly through the garden late the following morning. "I was so pleased when Beth told me of your engagement." She glanced over at her son. "You weren't going to keep it to yourself, were you?"

"Of course not," he answered, giving her a lazy smile. "You know Beth. She can't keep a secret." That was an easy explanation, he thought. He hoped his mother wouldn't ask too many questions. The long summer was more than enough time for her to catch small discrepancies, figure things out. "Besides," he added with a shrug as they continued down the garden path. "Kitty and I were only recently engaged."

"That explains the lack of an engagement ring, then."

Keefe went still. How had they overlooked that one important detail? A diamond ring—even a cheap fake—would have added indisputable credibility to their scam.

"Kitty's a very practical woman," he said, latching on to the first excuse that came to mind, hoping it would satisfy his mother. "Jewelry and other traditional symbols of devotion aren't that important to her."

"Nonsense!" Helen replied briskly, looking shocked at the very idea. "Practicality isn't the issue. Romance is. Every woman loves a diamond ring." With that opinion aired, she moved on to the end of the garden, making a sound of delight at the thick bank of deep purple and cream irises. "Harold has simply outdone himself with these bulbs! And they'll still be beautiful year after year."

Not if Wendell Burkett got his greedy hands on the property, Keefe thought, feeling his stomach tighten. It was time to bring the topic out in the open. "I was surprised to hear you put the manor on the market," he said carefully.

"What else am I going to do with a house that's too big for an old widow like me? You're busy at school. You rarely came home all last year," she pointed out. "The manor needs people. A family. Not a son who drops in for an occasional visit or a part-time caretaker past retirement age."

"Kitty and I would live here after we're married." His wistful tone caught him by surprise.

"You'd commute to Albany every day?"

"Absolutely. It's not a bad drive. I can make it in under an hour." He knew he had said the right thing, for his mother smiled and looked relieved.

"Well, then. That changes everything," Helen said with an enigmatic smile. "As long as I'm sure you and Kitty are right for each other. If not, it's pointless hanging on to this old estate."

Keefe decided he'd do whatever it took to convince her. Beth's scam had him feeling guilty as hell, but too much was at stake. He simply had no intention of letting Lakeview Manor slip into the hands of Wendell Burkett. If it took a whole summer of playing a phony fiancé, then so be it.

"I found it," Helen said triumphantly, breezing through the French doors leading from the dining room to the patio. She stopped directly in front of the cushioned bench where Kitty and Keefe were enjoying their after-dinner coffee.

Keefe set his cup down. "Found what, Mother?"

"This." Helen held up a small, brown leather box. Slowly she opened the lid. Inside, nestled on a bed of cream-colored velvet, was an antique gold diamond ring.

"Gram's ring!" Keefe said.

Helen offered the ring to Kitty. "It's yours."

"Oh, no." Kitty eyed the ring as if it had suddenly grown teeth. "I couldn't possibly take it!" She leaned back on the bench, glancing swiftly at Keefe for support.

Keefe should have known his mother wouldn't leave Kitty's lack of an engagement ring alone. "Perhaps Kitty would prefer something less traditional," he suggested.

"Oh, she *must* wear it! All Brody brides have worn this ring upon their betrothal!" Helen stared at her son, her eyes filled with censure. "It's a family tradition. Your grandmother and I have worn it. And your great-grandmother before that." She pressed the ring into Keefe's hand. "Please," she insisted. "You know, there is a legend associated with this ring. According to Keefe's great-grandmother, if the ring fits perfectly on the first try, it's a sign the marriage was meant to be."

Kitty's stomach fluttered a warning. She looked at Keefe, then at the ring, and held her breath. Of course, the ring wouldn't fit. How could it? Their engagement was a sham. And this marriage most definitely was *not* meant to be.

Keefe hesitated, then reached for Kitty's left hand. Slowly he slid the delicate gold band onto her third finger.

For a long moment no one spoke.

"What do you know," Keefe marveled softly, tracing a fingertip lightly around the ring. "It's a perfect

fit." He looked at her thoughtfully. "As if it was made
for you."

"The legend lives on," Helen whispered.

Kitty shivered. The evening air suddenly seemed
cool. Keefe shifted closer and placed an arm tenderly
around her shoulders. She leaned into him, staring
down at the ring gracing her finger. The diamond
was round and expertly cut, sparkling like a solitary
star, catching and reflecting the oranges and mauves
of the setting sun. The sight of it, the feel of the gold
band, warm against her skin, was eerie.

"That settles it," said Helen, looking pleased.
"Now your engagement is more official, don't you
think?"

Yes, Kitty agreed silently. More official. And oddly,
incredibly real. And while she knew it would have
pleased Beth to no end, all Kitty could feel was a
confusing mix of guilt and regret and aching need.

"We've got a problem," Kitty told Beth two days
later when they were alone in the solarium. She
flashed the bright diamond under Beth's nose. "This
ring is a perfect fit, and now your aunt thinks Keefe
and I are meant to be married."

"That's what we wanted her to think."

"But I'm wearing it under false pretenses. Thanks
to your scam, I'm making a mockery of everything
the ring stands for! I'm sure Keefe's ancestors are
turning in their graves."

Beth continued to gawk at the rock glittering on
Kitty's left hand. "I know it's all pretend," she con-

fessed in a quiet voice. "But that ring looks perfect on your hand. It belongs there." She gave a delicate shiver. "It's so romantic, Kitty! I get chills just looking at it."

Kitty folded her arms and quirked an eyebrow. "Then stop looking." She nodded toward the paint cans in the corner of the solarium. "Grab a brush and get busy. You can start priming the doorjambs while I work on this wainscot."

"Okay," Beth agreed absently. "But promise me you'll keep wearing the ring."

Kitty let out a weary breath. "Why? Your aunt already thinks we're really and truly engaged."

"I know. But think of the ring as a constant reminder. If she sees you've taken it off, she'll wonder if you're having second thoughts about the wedding." Beth put an urgent hand on Kitty's arm. "Spend every moment you can with Keefe. If Aunt Helen suspects what we're up to, she'll sell this place to Wendell Burkett in a heartbeat. Guaranteed."

Kitty sighed. If she let up now, the entire scam could blow up in their faces. And it would be all her fault.

She certainly didn't want that on her conscience.

So she did her part. She kept up appearances by wearing the ring everywhere, even though the distracting sparkle nearly had her hammering her thumb a few times. And just so Mrs. Brody wouldn't suspect anything, Kitty and Keefe took Beth's advice and made sure they were seen together every day.

But that part wasn't difficult. As the days passed, they quickly got into the habit of taking all their meals together. They were both early risers and more often than not found themselves alone at the breakfast table, talking quietly over a cup of coffee before starting their day. Lunches were spent with each other, too, as Beth usually headed out to meet Tom, and Helen preferred to lunch in town with her Garden Club friends.

Kitty, who had been known to skip lunch as a rule, now found herself looking forward to it. Keefe would pack a picnic basket with cold drinks, sandwiches and fresh fruit. They'd find a pretty spot down by the lake and watch the boats go by, then head slowly back to the house, pointing out various wildflowers along the way. Keefe could identify every tree, every flower, every bird in the Adirondack region, and his willingness to take the time to share his knowledge with her touched Kitty deeply.

Dinner was a time for easy laughter and spirited discussion. Beth loved to cook, though Kitty and Keefe and quite frequently Helen would be in the kitchen chopping vegetables or making a salad or teasing Beth good-naturedly about her culinary skills. When the dishes were done, they'd all take their coffee out on the patio. Then, while the sun eased down the mountains, Keefe and Kitty would go for a walk, strolling hand in hand through the garden. Even stealing a playful kiss, knowing Helen looked on.

Sometimes they'd wander down to the dock to watch the sun set over the lake, leaving when the night air turned cool and fireflies twinkled like scattered stars at the edge of the woods.

At least once a week they'd drive into town to catch

a movie or grab a quick bite to eat, as all engaged couples typically did. And they took advantage of the warm summer weather to do some serious sightseeing.

Keefe took Kitty to places he hadn't seen since he was a boy. Touristy places, like amusement parks and souvenir shops and local museums. He bought her a pair of soft, beaded moccasins and a lovely silver and turquoise bracelet. Plus his and her T-shirts, each with a grinning largemouth bass on the front.

As the summer days slipped into August, Kitty had to pinch herself to remember that her relationship with Keefe was really nothing but a sham. It had gotten so easy to pretend. It was so easy to act like they really had a future together, as if they were in love.

She shouldn't have let down her guard. She'd been drawn in by all the playacting, the easy companionship, the quiet moments, the shared laughter—all the little things they'd put into their relationship to make it look legitimate.

They'd been so busy fooling Helen Brody, Kitty had somehow managed to fool herself.

Keefe followed the tantalizing aroma of stir-fry into the kitchen. The wonderful smell had wafted into his study, luring him away from his desk. He found Kitty at the stove, poking at a sizzling concoction of shrimp and vegetables.

"Smells great." Keefe watched her stir vegetables with one hand and check beneath the lid of a steaming saucepan with the other. "My fiancée is a talented cook."

"I can't take credit for this. Beth did all the prep work." She gave him a quick smile. "Which was very nice of her considering she had a date with Tom tonight."

"Beth isn't here?" And his mother was at her annual Garden Club banquet, which tended to run late. Keefe shifted closer. "So . . . it's just you and me this evening?"

Kitty's heart gave an erratic thump. She shouldn't feel nervous at the prospect of a night alone with Keefe. They were both adults, after all. What could happen?

She blushed, trying to get suddenly explicit thoughts under control. She knew exactly what could happen. "Probably our last evening alone."

Keefe frowned. The month of August was flying by and their time together had dwindled to a mere handful of days. He'd known ever since the beginning that Kitty would leave one day. And life would return to normal.

He didn't want to go back to the way things were.

"Could you pour the wine?" Kitty shut off the burners and got out the serving dishes. "I think dinner's ready."

They dined by candlelight as night closed in around them, their conversation limited to casual chitchat. They poked at their food, neither one of them hungry, both all too aware their moments alone were drawing to a close.

After dinner they took their wine into the study.

Kitty kicked off her shoes, settling comfortably into the old leather couch while Keefe put on some soft music. She felt pleasantly drowsy, swirling the wine in her glass, watching the amber liquid sparkle in the lamplight.

Keefe dropped onto the sofa beside her and touched the edge of his glass to hers. "To us."

Their eyes locked as they sipped. In the background a tenor sax played slow, soft blues, mournful notes that made Kitty feel wistful. "You mean, the *pretend* us."

"I'm tired of pretending." He set his wine down and frowned. "It's been a long summer for playing games, Kitty."

"We're alone now, Keefe. You don't have to pretend."

Something flickered across his face as he raised his eyes to hers. "In other words, do what comes naturally." He took her glass and set it aside. Cupping her cheek in his hand, he whispered, "This comes naturally to me."

In the next instant his mouth was on hers, firm and warm and tasting of wine. Her lips parted, allowing his tongue to slip past. It moved in unison with hers, each sinuous caress making her senses spin.

Somehow she found the will to turn her head. "Keefe . . . we shouldn't. It's wrong." It had nothing to do with the success of the charade.

He nuzzled the side of her neck, his warm lips skimming down to her collarbone. "It doesn't feel wrong." He slipped his arms behind her waist, pulling her into his lap.

She started to protest but he was kissing her mouth again . . . deep, slow kisses that seemed to drug her. His hands skimmed around her waist, unsnapping her jeans, tugging her shirt free. Kitty moaned as he slipped his hands beneath her jeans, his fingers moving against the silken fabric of her panties, cupping her bottom, pressing her against him.

"We should stop," she whispered against his mouth. But instead of taking her own advice, she moved her hands along his shoulders to the nape of his neck, tangling her fingers in his hair, drawing him closer for another kiss. Her breasts moved against his chest, a delicious friction that made her breath catch. She didn't want to stop touching him. "You know I'm leaving soon . . ."

"You're here now," he said with a husky growl, nibbling lightly at her lower lip. His hands moved slowly up her bare back and around her rib cage, finding the front clasp of her bra. He paused, his fingers hovering over the delicate hook, while he leaned back to look at her. His eyes were heavy-lidded, smoky with passion. "So tell me to stop."

"Oh, Keefe . . ." She looked at him in despair. If this was still a game, she had stopped playing long ago. She was in love with him. She couldn't fool herself any more. The illusion had changed into something real and powerful, and it frightened her. He was still caught up in the game. And she'd be the one who'd end up hurt. "It's crazy for us to start something we can't finish."

Carefully he withdrew his hand from beneath her shirt and rose from the couch. Bending down, he scooped her up with an ease that made her pulse flare.

"What are you doing?" she gasped, looping her arms around his neck.

"Taking you someplace where we can finish."

He left the study and walked down the hallway. Kitty rested her head on his shoulder, feeling the slow, steady beat of his heart against her breast. Desire coursed through her veins when he began mounting the stairs to the bedrooms. She knew where he was going. Knew that he would finish what had started between them long before tonight. And suddenly, she didn't care if it was real or pretend.

One night. That's all she wanted. She would hold onto the memory, cherish it forever.

He entered his room and kicked the door shut behind him. The moon cast streaks of pale silver across the bed, and he carried her over, lowering her gently. For a moment he said nothing, his eyes shadowed and dark on her.

She felt chilled without him near. "Keefe . . ." She reached her hand through shafts of moonlight, catching his wrist. Her fingers closed around it and gave a gentle tug.

He groaned at the invitation and she felt the bed shift beneath his weight as he sat beside her. "I was half-afraid you'd tell me we were making a mistake."

Her eyes found his in the darkness. "It would be the best mistake I've ever made."

Keefe raised his hand, using the back of his fingers to lightly caress her cheek. He touched his thumb to her lower lip and rubbed gently. "Are you sure you want to be here? If we start this again, Kitty, I'm not sure I—"

She placed a fingertip softly against his mouth, silencing him. "I've never been more sure of anything," she whispered. "Let's have tonight, Keefe. Just one night."

Even in the cool light of the moon she saw hunger and desire burn a hot promise in his eyes, and her own needs flared an urgent response. He turned his face into her hand and kissed her palm, then leaned forward, capturing her mouth with his own. She gave a satisfied sigh and sank into his arms, her hands gripping the folds of his shirt, holding tight as she kissed him back.

"Wait . . ." he murmured. His eyes never leaving her, he unbuttoned his shirt, his slow, languid movements driving her crazy, heightening her arousal. With the last button undone, she reached out impatiently and pushed the shirt off his shoulders, running her hands back down over his warm, smooth flesh. She inched her fingers lower to unsnap his jeans, and hesitated. His moan of approval emboldened her. Slowly, inch by inch, she tugged the zipper down.

Standing, he shed his clothes. Moonlight spilled over him, making every taut muscle gleam like polished marble. He looked to Kitty like a living, breathing sculpture, an artist's rendition of the perfect male. Her heart pounded in anticipation as he drew her off the bed into his arms for one long, soul-searching kiss.

"Now you." He undid her blouse with deft fingers,

stripping it from her shoulders and dropping it to the floor. And then he was unfastening her jeans, helping her wriggle out of the tight denim, until she stood before him in nothing but pale silk and lace. His eyes darkened as he touched her gently, letting his fingers roam over her shoulders and down her back, then up again to the front clasp of her bra. With a slight twist of the hook, the delicate cups fell open, freeing her breasts.

"Wow . . ." he breathed, bending down to take one soft, full peak into his mouth, circling her hardening nipple with slow strokes of his tongue. Kitty arched her back, burying her fingers into his hair to press him closer.

With strong arms circling her waist, he lifted her up, settling her back on the bed. His fingers skimmed over her panties, catching the waistband, tugging it down until it, too, lay in the heap of discarded clothes on the floor.

She sighed with pleasure as his hands and mouth moved over her, teasing her, tasting her, his touch so gentle, so reverent, she could have wept for sheer joy. She had never experienced such overwhelming desire for a man.

He spent long, delicious moments kissing her breasts, then trailed his parted lips down to nuzzle the softness of her belly, and lower still, where his tongue, hot and wet, sought her most sensitive spot.

"Please . . ." Her voice caught with a desperate moan, and she clutched weakly at his shoulder. She couldn't wait any longer.

He reached across her and withdrew a foil packet

from the nightstand. Hating even the slightest interruption, she helped him rip it open, her hands trembling in her haste. When he was ready he settled himself between her thighs, giving her long, deep kisses that left them both breathless.

Finally, his gaze locked with hers, he eased himself slowly into her silken heat, and they moved together in unison, desire rekindled, building to a fevered pitch. The moonlight fractured into a thousand stars as sensation after sensation burst through Kitty. She wrapped her arms around Keefe, holding him close, his harsh groan of satisfaction echoing her own cry of delight. The world ceased to exist. Nothing else mattered. Nothing but the two of them, their soft moans of pleasure and the quiet whisper of flesh against flesh, a reality beyond their wildest dreams.

Dawn tinged the sky with streaks of pale pink. Kitty opened her eyes, feeling warm and drowsy in the shelter of Keefe's arms. She lay quietly, her back nestled against his chest, feeling the beat of his heart.

She had to go. Beth would be up soon, and Helen, too. Kitty didn't feel up to explanations, and Beth would want details. What could she say? That she'd gotten carried away? Gotten so caught up in the illusion she didn't know what was real anymore? How complicated everything had become!

She eased herself from Keefe's embrace, careful not to awaken him. The morning air chilled her bare skin. She wanted nothing more than to climb back into bed, feel his warm flesh against her own. But the

night was over. The rules were different in the light
of day. They'd go back to the game, back to the roles
they had to play.

Her heart aching, she gathered her clothes and
crept across the hall to her room. She had wanted
one night with Keefe. And she had gotten it.

But one night would never be enough.

The last-minute faculty meeting couldn't have
come at a worse time. Keefe shifted in the auditorium
seat, trying without success to keep his attention on
the podium up front. Philip Martin, Dean of Aca-
demic Services, was giving an endless fiscal report in
his usual monotone.

Keefe hated spending a single hour away from
Kitty. He had come to treasure their moments together. With the end of summer looming ever closer,
they didn't have much time left. The thought of
Lakeview Manor without Kitty had him aching with
loneliness. She'd brought new life to the empty
rooms, like a ray of spring sunshine after a long, cold
winter.

He closed his eyes against the drone of the dean's
voice, thinking of last night, remembering her soft
cries of pleasure, how the moon had gleamed against
her body, the softness of her skin beneath his hands.
She had responded to him with an intensity that had
stunned him, taking his passion and giving it back in
equal amounts.

The auditorium erupted in sudden laughter.
Keefe's eyes snapped open. He blinked and looked

around. Apparently, he had missed one of Martin's amusing anecdotes. Biting back a curse, he grabbed a pencil and paper from his briefcase, ready to take notes. But after suffering through five more minutes of the dean's report, he found himself doodling instead, filling the entire page with rough pencil sketches of Kitty's pretty face.

The meeting adjourned after two interminable hours. Keefe gathered his briefcase, making small talk with his colleagues as they made their way to the exit. But before he could get to the door, the dean had stepped down from the podium and pulled him aside, seeking privacy. "I need to have a word with you."

Keefe eyed the thin, gray-haired man, trying to crush his rising impatience. He was eager to return home to Kitty. "What can I do for you, Philip?"

The dean waited until the auditorium emptied, then adjusted his glasses, looking serious. "As you know, Keefe, I'm the designated ombudsman for the university," he began carefully. "We receive a variety of complaints and it's my job to investigate each and every one of them."

Keefe didn't say anything, but simply stared at the dean, waiting for him to get to the point.

Martin cleared his throat. "We've received a complaint about you."

Keefe's eyes narrowed. "From whom?"

"He wouldn't say." Martin paused while a maintenance man noisily wheeled the podium from center stage. "But he accused you of unethical conduct, Keefe. Insisted that any professor involved in a fraudulent scheme over real estate shouldn't be teaching impressionable young adults."

Everything inside Keefe went cold. Suddenly it was plain what the accusation was all about. Jay Hilliard. It had to have been Hilliard who placed the call. He had sworn he'd get even, and he did.

He sighed. It was time to come clean. "Listen, Phil," he said, suddenly weary of the whole charade. "I'd better explain." Briefly, he filled the dean in on all the details.

"Wendell Burkett?" Martin repeated when Keefe had finished explaining. "That's impossible. He couldn't buy Lakeview Manor, let alone a cup of coffee. He's been in prison for the last three years. Tax evasion, racketeering, insurance fraud, you name it." He peered at Keefe through his bifocals. "Didn't you know that?"

Keefe didn't answer, feeling oddly numb. *Prison,* he told himself calmly. *The man's been in prison . . .*

Martin was looking at him with a strange smile. "Just who is being conned here, Keefe?"

Ten

Keefe pulled into the driveway at Lakeview Manor just as a light rain began to fall. He remembered nothing of the drive home, following the same route he'd taken countless times, responding automatically to traffic and the familiar twists and turns of the road.

His mind had been occupied with other things.

What a fool he'd been. There had never been any threat from Wendell Burkett. Or *any* realtor. He and Kitty had been duped into a pretend engagement. Plain and simple.

Hell, he thought as he climbed out of his Jeep. Maybe he should thank Jay Hilliard for bringing it all out into the open. Hilliard's retaliation had been a blessing in disguise. If it hadn't been for Philip Martin's knowledge of Wendell Burkett, the scam would have gone on forever.

The scam. His mother may have been involved in it, but Keefe could bet the idea wasn't hers. Oh, no. This was Beth's specialty. It had her imprint all over it. It was a classic double cross.

Beth had used his fear of losing the manor, conned Kitty into the game, convinced his mother to go along with it, then sat back while they played right into her hands.

The question was, *why?*

Why was a pretend engagement so important to Beth?

Hunching his shoulders against the rain, he headed around back to the kitchen door, pausing to wipe his damp shoes on the mat. It was quiet inside, the gathering clouds casting the house in gray shadows. Keefe headed down the hallway, hoping everyone was home. He'd need all the players assembled for the finale to Beth's little show.

As luck would have it, they were all in the solarium. Beth and Helen were busy rearranging the wrought iron furniture. Kitty was moving a huge ficus tree into place in the corner. There was a frown of concentration on her face, her lower lip caught between her teeth as she slid the earthen pot with extra care over the polished brick floor.

She looked up, smiling when she saw him, and his heart turned over just as it had done the very first time she had smiled at him. "How was your meeting?"

"Very enlightening." He hesitated, knowing that Beth's scam would hurt Kitty the most. "I learned an interesting bit of news about Wendell Burkett."

He walked over to Beth, noting her quick look of apprehension. Then she began fussing with the cushions on the chaise, plumping them up, patting them down, her hands moving restlessly. "Oh?" Beth tried to smile.

"You had me convinced I could lose the manor to

him. And the only way to stop it was an engagement. A phony one."

He heard Kitty's soft intake of breath, knew she was shocked to hear him bring the scam into the open. "It might have worked, too," he continued. "If I hadn't found out that Burkett hasn't been in the real estate business lately."

"He is, too!" Beth argued. "Where else would he be?"

"In prison."

Beth's face turned pale. "I—I don't know what you're talking about."

"It's obvious you don't. And that's where you went wrong." He stared at his cousin until her cheeks turned red. "Let me fill you in," he said with exaggerated patience. "Burkett was convicted of quite a list of things. Insurance fraud, racketeering, tax evasion, just to name a few. If you *had* known that, you wouldn't have used him as a threat."

Beth fumbled for an explanation while Kitty went wide-eyed with shock and disbelief. "I don't know where you got your information, but—"

"From a reliable source."

"Well, it's wrong. Wendell called just last week, and—"

"Stop it, Beth," Helen finally cut in with a sigh. "It's no use. We obviously didn't plan well enough. It never occurred to me to check into Wendell Burkett a little more thoroughly. I just assumed he was still building those atrocious developments."

Keefe turned toward his mother, his eyes narrowing. "So, this was *your* idea?"

Beth was quick to take the blame. "The idea was mine," she admitted in a subdued voice, her shoulders drooping under the weight of her confession. "I talked your mother into it." She stared miserably at her cousin. "I didn't mean any harm, Keefe. Honest I didn't."

"You never do, Beth," he said testily. He raked a hand through his hair, torn between anger and compassion. Beth was always sorry. After the fact. "But you never think about who might get hurt before you act."

Her gaze faltered and she stared at the floor. For a long moment no one spoke. The only sound came from the rain, a soft, pattering noise against the roof, a sound Keefe normally would have found soothing. Now, though, his nerves felt as tight as a bowstring.

"Would you mind telling me the point of all this?" he finally asked. "Why con two people who didn't even know each other into a pretend engagement?"

Beth shot him a defiant look. "Because it was the only way I could get you two together!"

Keefe's expression turned incredulous. "This was all just a ploy to get us to spend time with each other?"

"Yes!" She stepped closer to Keefe, her hands jammed at her waist. "It was so obvious right from the start you were perfect for each other! But you both refused to see that. You both wanted nothing to do with each other!"

Keefe couldn't believe what he was hearing. "I spent the summer playing a silly game just so you could dabble in matchmaking. It was nothing but a huge waste of time."

"All your relationships are a waste of time!"

Keefe flinched at the deliberate gibe. He didn't need to be reminded of the parade of women he had dated over the years. He glanced over his shoulder at Kitty. She was staring at the floor, looking as though she wanted to cry. He sighed heavily and turned back to Beth.

"How do you think Kitty feels now that she knows her best friend has lied to her all summer?"

Beth winced, the question hitting her like a slap.

Helen moved forward and laid a gentle hand on her son's arm. "This has turned into such a mess," she admitted. "And I'm sorry. We only had the best intentions."

"Best for whom?"

"Why, for both of you, of course. Beth was so certain you and Kitty were meant for each other. She was desperate enough to try something a little . . . outlandish. She asked for my help and I gave it. I trusted her judgment. As soon as I saw you and Kitty together, well . . . I knew Beth was right." Helen turned to look at Kitty. "That's strange," she said with a frown. "She was just here a minute ago."

Keefe moved to go after her, but Beth stopped him. "Give me some time with her, Keefe," she said quietly. "I've got a lot of explaining to do."

Waste of time . . . silly game . . . Kitty swallowed against the lump in her throat as she tossed her lingerie into the suitcase lying on the bed. She jerked open the drawer containing her T-shirts and took them out in one big bundle, throwing them on top of her other clothes, too irritable to care if they stayed neatly folded.

Her gaze settled on the souvenir T-shirt that Keefe had bought her. Gently she smoothed out a wrinkle, her eyes prickling with tears at the sight of the large-mouth bass, grinning up at her as if at some joke.

Talk about a joke, she thought bitterly. It had all been a joke. The threat to Lakeview Manor. The need for a convincing engagement. The begging. The pleading. The phony tears. All of it. One big, long, practical joke.

And she'd been taken in by it.

She still couldn't believe it. Couldn't believe Beth, her best friend, had set her up like this.

Learn all you can about him, she'd insisted. *Spend time with him. Act like you're in love. Kiss him, for effect.*

Very funny.

Thinking about it made Kitty feel cold and sick. She walked quickly to the closet, yanking shirts and jeans off hangers, shoving them in with her other clothes. She had a lot of things to pack. She intended to be gone by nightfall.

A loud knock at the door made her jump nervously. She ignored it and kept packing. The door opened a moment later and Beth poked her head into the room. "We need to talk."

"I can't imagine what needs to be said at this point, Beth." Kitty turned to grab an empty suitcase. She unzipped it and laid it on the bed next to the other one, packing away pajamas and sweatshirts. Her robe. Slippers. The beaded moccasins Keefe had purchased at the village trading post.

She picked one up, running a finger over the leather fringe and the colorful beads and nearly started crying.

Beth came in the rest of the way, her eyes widening in alarm. "You—you can't be leaving! Not now. Not yet!"

"Why not?" Kitty continued putting clothes away, refusing to show Beth just how deeply she'd been hurt. "I'm done in the west wing. A full week ahead of schedule, too. Even though I was distracted with other . . . circumstances."

Beth's eyes were bleak. "Please don't go. I—I want to explain everything—"

"There's no need. I think I've heard enough." She shook out a cotton pullover, refolded it, and laid it neatly on top of her robe. "I have to admit, though, you really pulled one over on me. This was your best practical joke ever."

"It wasn't meant to be a joke!"

"You're right," Kitty said with a false, bright smile. "No one seems to be laughing."

Beth watched helplessly as Kitty continued packing. "You don't understand why I . . . why I did what I did."

"I don't understand a lot of things, Beth," Kitty said, lifting her hand in a gesture of resignation. "Did you think we would never find out?"

"I knew you'd find out eventually," Beth admitted. "But I was sure by the time you did you'd be so much in love that you wouldn't care." She moved in front of Kitty, blocking her path to the closet. "I knew that if you two would only spend time together, you'd end up falling in love."

"Well, you were wrong."

"I don't believe you."

A ghost of a smile touched Kitty's mouth. "It appears you've been fooled by your own scam."

"Baloney! I know you're in love with Keefe. You can deny it all you want. But I've never seen you look at any man the way you look at him. Not even the man you married!"

Kitty turned away, embarrassed. Beth's assessment had been dead-on. "I didn't realize it was that obvious." Who else had noticed? Keefe?

Oh, Lord, she thought, closing her eyes. The memory of their lovemaking surged to the surface. She had fallen in love with a man whose feelings for her were only as real as the game they had played. A game he himself had declared was a waste of time.

The brutal reminder nearly had her doubling over in pain. How could she ever face him again?

Well, she wouldn't. She planned to be home before he even missed her. A small voice inside called her a coward for running away. The need for self-preservation overruled.

"It doesn't make any difference what I feel," she said, quietly. "The game's over. Time to go our separate ways."

Beth sniffled as genuine tears started to roll down her cheeks. "At least talk with Keefe. He's in love with you."

Kitty raised an eyebrow at that remark. "Come on, Beth," she said with mild reproof. "Don't read anything else into it. Keefe was doing exactly what you told him to do—playing the enamored groom-to-be. Nothing more, nothing less."

Beth swiped at her tears. "It wasn't an act!"

Kitty snorted in disbelief as she stuffed the last of her clothes in the suitcase and zipped it shut. But she had to admit he *had* played the role quite convincingly.

"Well," she said, giving the room a last look. "I guess that's everything. Oh, I almost forgot." She twisted the antique diamond ring off her finger and placed it on the dresser. Odd that she had grown so accustomed to wearing it. "Can't walk off with one of the props, can I?" She grabbed her suitcases and headed out.

"Kitty, wait—"

But Kitty had no intention of waiting. Her mind was made up. She headed down the stairs and outside into the gray dusk, leaving Beth no choice but to follow.

Rain still fell, fat drops splashing in puddles on the glossy black driveway. Keeping her face tucked down, Kitty hurried to her truck to load up the suitcases, ignoring the pleas and apologies tumbling nonstop from Beth's lips as she trailed behind.

"I'm so sorry, Kitty." Raindrops mingled with her tears. "Can you forgive me?"

Kitty sighed as she looked at the friend who had been by her side through thick and thin. Her woeful expression tore at her heart. She could never stay mad at Beth. After all these years, one thing stayed the same: Beth always meant well.

"I forgive you." She patted her friend on the shoulder. "Look at us—we're getting soaked! I've got to go. Please tell your aunt good-bye for me."

"Let me go get Keefe—"

"No!" Kitty opened her car door and climbed behind the wheel. "I . . . I don't think I can see him again." She knew if she didn't leave soon, she'd start sobbing hysterically. Her heart already felt broken in two. She started the engine. "Tell him I . . . wish him all the luck for the future. And if he's ever in Philadelphia—" She broke off on a sob.

The message had sounded superficial and impersonal. And not at all what was in her heart.

She blinked back the tears blurring her eyes and waved good-bye to Beth.

"She *left?*" Keefe had come upstairs looking for Kitty and had found Beth alone, staring broodingly at the diamond ring Kitty had left behind. He felt a cold lump settle in his stomach. "When?"

Beth sighed sadly as she put the ring down. "A half-hour ago."

Keefe frowned. He'd had no idea when Kitty walked out of the solarium that she'd be walking out of his life. "Why didn't you come get me? I would have stopped her."

"She didn't want you to know." Beth sat on the edge of the bed and began fussing with the flounces on the coverlet, avoiding his eyes. "I can't say any more," she declared primly. "I think I've caused enough trouble already."

Keefe was beside her in an instant. "Dammit, Beth. This is no time to develop a conscience! Why did she leave? Doesn't she know I'm in love with her?"

His words had the effect of a trumpet blast. Beth leapt to her feet, overjoyed. "I knew it! I *knew* you were in love with her! I tried to tell her that, but of course she wouldn't listen. She felt just awful being so in love with you when—*oops!*" Beth clapped a hand over her mouth.

Keefe grinned. "That's all I wanted to hear." With purposeful strides, he headed to his room and got out a suitcase.

Beth followed, watching in amazement as he started packing. "You're going? Now?"

"I'll leave first thing in the morning." He grabbed his shaving kit and tossed it in with his clothes. "I plan to be in Philadelphia before noon. Kitty and I always have lunch together and I'm not about to stop now."

The blaring of a car horn awakened Kitty. Unaccustomed to the loud noise, she bolted up, blinking her eyes at the bright, late-morning sunshine. She felt disoriented, as if she couldn't quite remember where she was. Humid August air floated through the open window by her bed, bringing a blast of hot asphalt and bus fumes that burned her nose.

Ugh. She remembered where she was now.

Grimacing, she climbed out of bed and headed

into the kitchen for a light breakfast of tea and toast. Not even back a day and already she missed the cool, pine-scented freshness of the Adirondacks.

And, she realized with a sharp pang of loneliness, Keefe.

Back in Lake George, she would have been checking her watch about now, counting the hours till lunch with Keefe. They'd carry the picnic basket and blanket down to the lake and pick out a nice spot beneath a shade tree, watch the sun sparkle off the water, listen to the soothing, lazy sound of gentle waves lapping the shore—

She stopped the daydream from going any further. Those days were over. She would *not* live in the past and moon over a man who didn't love her. No matter how much she loved him.

With that resolution made, she finished her breakfast and tidied up her small kitchen.

The cashier placed the sandwiches, cookies and juice boxes in the bag. "Will that be all, sir?" she asked, tossing the fringe of auburn bangs out of her eyes.

Keefe nodded and drew the required amount of money out of his wallet. "I need to find Lombard Street," he said.

"Head south." She chewed and snapped the wad of pink gum in her mouth as she considered her answer. "Six or seven blocks past Market. Can't miss it."

Twenty minutes later, he parked in front of Kitty's apartment building, his heart hammering at the base

of his throat. He felt as nervous as a kid on his first
date.

He looked at his watch. Almost noon. He couldn't
have timed it more perfectly.

He unpacked the sandwiches and the other items
purchased from the deli and placed them in the picnic basket he had brought with him from Lake
George. Then with a final glance at his watch, he
walked toward the building.

Kitty stared into her empty refrigerator. She'd have
to go grocery shopping if she wanted any lunch. Or
starve. She shut the refrigerator door and checked
her cupboards, finding a box of crackers that were
undoubtedly stale.

She tossed them in the trash. There was absolutely
nothing to eat.

She was about to grab her purse when someone
knocked on the door.

Kitty frowned. It must be her landlord, she thought
as she walked to the door and opened it. But she
found her pulse fluttering and her knees wobbling
at the sight of the man standing there.

"Keefe!" she murmured. He was *here*. In Philadelphia. Her gaze roamed over him as if she could
hardly believe her eyes, lingering on the neat white
T-shirt that hugged his broad shoulders, the jeans
sunfaded to a soft, pale blue. She gestured for him
to enter. "What are you doing here?" He was the last
person she had expected to see.

He held up his picnic basket and followed her inside. "It's lunchtime. Don't we usually spend it together?"

She stared at the basket and then at him, not knowing what to make of the situation. He had driven nearly three hundred miles for lunch? "But . . . it took you hours to get here. You came all this way just to take me to lunch?"

"Yeah," he answered with a shrug, stepping into her little kitchen to set the picnic basket on the table. He turned back to her. "Is there something wrong with that?"

"I—I just . . ." She looked at him in bewilderment, her hands coming to life, making small, nervous gestures as she talked. "Lunch was just a . . . a ruse," she argued. "For your mother's sake. Now that we don't need to pretend, I'm sure you—"

She broke off as Keefe suddenly grabbed her hands and held them still. She gazed at him in silence for a moment.

"I was right," he said, smiling down at her. "You can't talk without your hands moving."

She pulled her hands from his grasp, looking more amused than embarrassed. "You've come to make fun of me."

"It's one of the things I find irresistible about you."

It made her smile. And the heat in his eyes warmed her to her very toes. "Did Beth put you up to this?"

"Beth who?" he growled, then reached out to pull her into his arms. "From now on I listen only to Kitty O'Neill." He gave her a quick, hard kiss. "I've missed you."

Kitty let out a soft laugh and placed her hands

lightly on his chest, gazing up into the deep green of his eyes. "I haven't even been gone a day."

"It felt like forever. You didn't have to leave just because Beth's little scheme came to a surprising end."

Kitty's eyes narrowed and she shifted in his arms. "How did you find out the truth about Wendell Burkett, anyway?"

He gave her an enigmatic smile. "We have your ex-husband to thank for that particular good deed."

"Jay?" she asked, eyeing him skeptically. "Jay Hilliard has never done a good deed in his life!"

"This time he did. Unintentionally, I'm sure." He told Kitty about the anonymous phone call to the university, and the subsequent revelation of Wendell Burkett's whereabouts. "So it was Hilliard who indirectly tipped Beth's hand."

"Poor Jay," Kitty said. "He meant to get even, but he did us a favor." She smiled and looped her arms around Keefe's waist. "I'll be sure to send him a thank you note."

Keefe chuckled and lowered his forehead to lightly press against hers. "I have a confession to make."

"What is it?" She braced herself for his answer. Expected him to tell her that this lunch would be their last. That it was fun while it lasted, but she'd never see him again after today.

"The whole time we were pretending to like each other?"

"Yes?" She bit her lip. Her breath seemed to be stuck in her lungs.

"I wasn't pretending," he said quietly. "I've been

in love with you all summer." He cleared his throat and eased back, his eyes locked with hers. "Come back to New York with me, Kitty. I want you to be my fiancée again."

Her face flushed with happiness at his words but she couldn't suppress a note of mischief in her voice. She stepped back from him and put her hands on her hips. "Would this be a real proposal?"

He dug inside his pocket. "Will this make it official?"

Kitty's eyes widened at the sight of the glittering diamond. "Your grandmother's ring!"

"I'd like it to be yours." He cupped her cheek in his hand. "I thought I couldn't bear to lose Lakeview Manor. But it's you I don't want to lose. That old house means nothing without you, Kitty." His eyes held hers. For a moment she didn't speak and he was filled with the very real fear that she might turn him down. But in the next instant she was smiling softly.

"I have a confession to make, too. But I think you already know what it is."

"Will I like it?"

"Only if you like hearing me say I love you."

He smiled and drew her back into his arms. "I could get used to it," he drawled, dropping his mouth down on hers for a gentle kiss. "Does this mean you'll come back to Lake George and marry me?"

"All you have to do is ask."

Tenderly, he took her left hand in his. "Will you marry me, Kitty O'Neill?"

She gazed up at him, at the man she had come to

love through the most unusual of circumstances, and said simply, "Yes."

Solemnly, he slipped the antique ring on her finger. "Still a perfect fit," he said, then laughed as he swept her up into his arms. "I love you, lady."

Grinning, she circled her arms around his neck and hugged him close. "No fooling, Keefe," she said, sighing. "No fooling."